THE Amaranth ENCHANTMENT

THE Amaranth ENCHANTMENT

~ JULIE BERRY ~

BLOOMSBURY

NEW YORK BERLIN LONDON

Published by Bloomsbury U.S.A. Children's Books
175 Fifth Avenue, New York, New York 10010

Library of Congress Cataloging-in-Publication Data
Berry, Julie.
The Amaranth enchantment / Julie Berry.—1st U. S. ed.
p.   cm.
Summary: Orphaned at age five, Lucinda, now fifteen, stands with courage against the
man who took everything from her, aided by a thief, a clever goat, and a mysterious
woman called the Witch of Amaranth, while the prince she knew as a child prepares to
marry, unaware that he, too, is in danger.
ISBN-13: 978-1-59990-334-7 • ISBN-10: 1-59990-334-2
[1. Fantasy.   2. Orphans—Fiction.   3. Princes—Fiction.   4. Extraterrestrial
beings—Fiction.]   I. Title.
PZ7.B461747Amc 2009   [Fic]—dc22   2008022354

First U.S. Edition 2009
Book design by Donna Mark
Typeset by Westchester Book Composition
Printed in the U.S.A. by Quebecor World Fairfield
2 4 6 8 10 9 7 5 3

For Jack, for Plum,
and always,
for Phil

THE Amaranth ENCHANTMENT

Amaranth

Immortal amarant, a flower which once
In Paradise, fast by the tree of life,
Began to bloom; but soon for man's offence
To Heaven removed, where first it grew, there grows,
And flowers aloft shading the fount of life,
And where the river of bliss through midst of Heaven
Rolls o'er Elysian flowers her amber stream;
With these that never fade the Spirits elect
Bind their resplendent locks.

—Milton, *Paradise Lost*, iii, 353–361

Prologue

I sit on a velvet stool at Mama's feet, watching her brush her hair.

I don't like brushing my hair. Nurse yanks the snarls, and it hurts. But when Mama brushes hers with slow, smooth strokes, it spills like chocolate over her milk white shoulders.

Nurse wants to put me to bed, but Mama is going to a ball tonight, and she says I can stay up to watch her get ready. I am five years old.

Mama flicks her hair toward me like a horse's tail. It tickles my face. Anna, her maid, wrestles with her heavy hair the way Cook battles with brown bread dough. I play with Mama's tin of lilac-scented powder and wait for Anna to finish weaving in strands of tiny pearls.

At last Mama turns to me. "Well?"

"You look like a fairy queen," I say.

She smiles. "Then you're my pixie."

Papa comes in and fastens the clasp of Mama's necklace. A net of emeralds and gold unfolds at her throat. Papa kisses her neck, then stands back to admire her. Mama brushes the stones with her fingertips.

"Someday, Lucinda," she says, "these jewels will all be yours."

"I already have some," I say, pointing to a gold charm bracelet around my wrist.

They smile, kiss me, and hurry down the hall, warning me to be good for Nurse. Papa, so tall and handsome. Mama, sparkling and trailing perfume.

They leave for the ball.

But they never come back.

Chapter 1

I was sweeping the shop when a glimmer between two floorboards caught my eye. A penny? I knelt for a closer look.

With a fingernail I pried out a grimy length of delicate chain. I rubbed it between my fingers. Gold! I tugged until it popped loose, then moved to the window for better light.

My heart beat faster. Just a short length of kinked chain, broken in the middle. Near the clasp, clotted with dust, was a tiny pendant. I bit my lip and polished the dirt away.

I knew it, even after ten years. A golden rose enameled red. My eyes misted over.

Aunt appeared at my side. "What's that you got there?"

I closed my fingers over the bracelet.

"It's mine," I said. "From when I was little. I just found it in the floorboards."

She held out a hand. "Give it to me."

Oh, why didn't I think to conceal it from her? "It's mine! My parents gave it to me."

She paid no heed, but pried my fingers apart and snatched the bracelet. She dangled it in front of her nose. I watched, fuming. Could she never let me have something of my own, even something so small as a happy memory?

"Shoddy work," she pronounced. "I'd have thought your parents could have afforded better. Still," she dropped it into her pocket, "it'll clean up enough to sell when Ernest repairs it."

I knew what would come of it, but I was too angry to care. "That bracelet belongs to me," I said. "You can't have it."

Aunt took a step closer.

"Listen here, my girl," she said. "Nothing belongs to you. This trinket," she patted her pocket, "is a tiny payment on all you owe us for your keep. Seems you need a reminder of that."

Next would come the wallop. I braced myself.

The bell on the door jingled, and Aunt froze. In a wink she had on her storefront smile, and the hand that was about to slap me was patting my shoulder. Harder than necessary.

A woman entered the shop. She was tall and slim and dressed in a gray cloak with a hood that hid most of her pale face. The wind swirled around her as she entered, even for a moment after the door shut.

"How may I assist you, Madam?" Aunt said in her customer voice as she slid back behind the counter. I jabbed at the corner with my broom.

The woman approached Aunt.

"I am in somewhat of a hurry." Her speech was refined, with an accent I couldn't label. "I need a new setting for this." She opened her hand.

Aunt sucked in her breath. In spite of myself I edged toward the counter for a better look.

In the woman's smooth palm lay the largest gem I'd seen in ten years of hovering around Uncle's goldsmith's shop. It was perfectly round and smooth, about the size of a walnut, and milky white, though its surface glinted with reflected colors.

People just didn't bring gems like that into Montescue's Goldsmithy. Aunt's eyes bulged.

"Is it a pearl?" I asked.

The lady turned her gaze my way. She blinked as if startled.

Aunt hissed through her teeth at me, then favored her customer with an oily smile. "Pardon our servant," she said, her voice dripping like honey. "She's an ignorant, presumptuous girl who forgets her place."

As if I could forget my miserable place.

The woman studied me up and down. Was I dirty? I brushed off my apron.

"I see," she said. She turned to Aunt. "Can you create a

new setting for this so I may wear it on a chain as before?"

"Certainly," Aunt said. "Although . . . how shall I say . . . this is an unusual piece. So splendidly large! The amount of gold it will take, and the challenge of setting a round stone without facets . . ." She coughed lightly.

The woman pulled a purse from within her cloak and poured out a pile of gold pieces on the counter. "I am prepared to pay whatever is needed."

Aunt's eyes gleamed as she watched the woman scoop the coins back into her purse. "We are most gratified, Madam, that you have entrusted Montescue's with this precious ornament! I assure you, no detail will be spared." She smiled the closed-lip smile that hid her terrible teeth. "If you'll just sign your name and address in our book, we'll contact you when the setting is finished." She pushed the red leather volume toward the lady, who dipped the pen in the ink and wrote.

Aunt made a show of squinting at the writing. "I've forgotten my spectacles. What is your name, Madam?" Aunt did not own spectacles, nor could she read.

"Beryl," the woman said, her hand on the door.

No surname, I noticed. Strange. She looked at me again, which gave me a curious, goose-pimply feeling, as if she could read my thoughts.

For the first time, I noticed her eyes. They gave me a pang, they were so lovely, wide and deep and long lashed.

Like something I might have seen once in a dream of a guardian angel. I had to force myself not to stare.

To Aunt, the woman said, "If you'll pardon the question, I am in need of a servant. I would gladly rid you of this 'presumptuous' girl and take her in hand myself."

Aunt's gracious-for-customers face curdled. She blinked rapidly.

Take me in hand? I wasn't a dog in need of training. Servant to a wealthy lady? My parents had such servants once. If my parents were still alive, I'd have a lady's maid myself right now.

But they weren't, and I didn't.

It seemed likely this Beryl would feed me and unlikely she'd beat me. If she did slap, slim as she was, her wallops shouldn't sting so much as Aunt's. I nearly let myself hope.

Beryl continued. "I would offer a fee for your inconvenience, to help find a replacement."

She really wanted me. Whatever for?

Aunt's mouth opened and shut. I wanted to laugh. I could practically see the wheels spinning in her head. What to say now? That they couldn't get on without me? That I wasn't, in fact, a servant but unpaid almost-kin? That they couldn't afford to hire a paid servant? But she wouldn't dare offend the lady. Perhaps she *would* sell me. And how would that feel?

As of this moment, just fine.

Aunt wasn't my real aunt, nor Uncle Ernest my uncle,

though once he was, back when he was married to my mother's sister, Evangeline, who died. Evidently I took after Evangeline in face, which didn't help my cause with Aunt. Since my parents died and Uncle took me in, she had soothed her itch by tormenting me daily. But there we were, until I saw my way clear to supporting myself.

Such as by finding employment as a servant. Why not? At fifteen, I was ready.

I looked up at Beryl and Aunt, who were still locked in a staring match.

Beryl spoke before Aunt could answer. "I apologize. It was presumptuous of me to ask. We'll say no more about it." And with a small bow, she withdrew and shut the door. *Thunk* went the door against the jamb, and *poof* went my little flicker of hope.

I watched the woman's back disappear down the street.

"Is she gone?" Aunt asked, breathless. I nodded.

"Ernest!" she shrilled, grabbing the gem and running toward the stairs. She halted in the doorway and turned. I looked down. I'd hoped she had forgotten.

Aunt closed the distance between us in two steps and clouted my ears.

Slap.

"That's for speaking out of turn," she said, and *slap.* "That's for making eyes at her so she'd want you. As if anybody would. A fine spectacle you made of yourself. And this"—*slap, slap*—"is for crossing me over this insignificant rubbish."

Meaning my bracelet.

She turned and vanished through the doorway to the kitchen and on up the stairs.

At least she'd gotten both sides evenly. I rubbed my ears. They felt hot.

I let a couple of tears fall. Not for the slaps. She couldn't hurt me there. I cried for the bracelet, and for Mama and Papa, and for the friendless days on end that I'd spent in this wretched shop without being able to recall their faces. The bracelet had given me a fleeting memory, sweet as candy, until she snatched it away.

No, not quite friendless. Uncle was kind, in his way. But he couldn't shield me from Aunt's spite—no more than he could shield himself.

I wiped my eyes and rubbed my face and put my sorrows back where they belonged.

In the rare moments such as these when I was alone in the shop, I liked to pretend it was mine. I took my rag and stood behind the counter, polishing its glass surface. Inside, on red velvet faded to brown, sat the few forlorn little ornaments that Uncle kept for sale. Mostly he did goldsmithing work to order, repairing belt buckles and hair clips for folks who came in, but he kept a scant inventory of dusty, outmoded pieces. The days when Montescue's was a fashionable, prosperous jewelry store were gone.

There was one piece I loved, a garnet ring. Easily the finest piece we had, if only a garnet. Sometimes Uncle let me slip it on when Aunt was out. I rubbed out a smudge in the glass over where it stood in state among the other tawdry trinkets, and dreamed it was my own.

The bell tinkled. Twice in one morning! I looked up.

A handsomely dressed young man came in looking bewildered, as if he'd taken the wrong turn on Jericho Street. He consulted a card in his hand. At the sight of the shabby store his face fell, but he entered anyway, apparently determined to make the best of it. Twice he looked over his shoulder and out the window, as if hoping to avoid being seen.

When his eyes adjusted to the dim light, he noticed me for the first time and smiled.

I stared and forgot to curtsy. Underneath his broad-brimmed hat, his features were so noble and fine, he looked like he'd swallowed the sun for breakfast.

He approached the counter. "Good day," he said. "I'm hoping you can help me find something very special." He smiled, showing his dimples.

I couldn't resist. "How special?" Was *I* being coy with a customer?

He dimpled even more. "Very special. A gift for a lady, as it happens."

Ask a foolish question, Lucinda.

"Something unusual, something that says . . ." He gazed upward, gesturing melodramatically, ". . . forever."

Twang went my heartstrings. Forever. Even if I wasn't the lady in question, I was charmed, and not just by his unnerving beauty. There was more to his eyes than sparkle—something pure and hopeful, like a boy picking flowers for his mother. It made me trust him right down to my toenails.

"A gift that says 'forever,'" I repeated slowly. "Well, the goldsmith could engrave the word 'forever' on the back of something, but that would cost extra. . . ."

"No, no, no." He looked flustered for a moment, then relaxed. "You're teasing me."

"I? Never." I smiled at him, far longer than I should have. But the pleasure of seeing him smile back made me forget everything I ought to remember, including his special lady.

His lady. Was I fool enough to think he'd come in for the pleasure of smiling at me? Fool enough to imagine, maybe. But he was a customer. He lived to be served.

"What do you have in mind, sir?" I asked. "We have some very nice combs over here, inlaid with mother-of-pearl." I traced my fingers along the counter. "And here we have some lovely cameos, just what a lady would want. They can be worn on a pin, chain, or ribbon."

I came to the garnet ring. It pained me, but I said it.

"Here's a pretty ring. Red, the color of love." Also, I was sure, the color of my face.

He bent to examine it, and frowned. "Do you think it says 'Forever'?"

I began to wish that a hive of hornets might visit his

special lady, or that perhaps her ankles would swell after eating strawberries.

"Don't you suppose it depends upon the lady? You must know something of her tastes."

He shook his head. "That's just it. I know nothing of them."

His eyes were so beseeching that I yearned to help him, even if it was to woo some plump, spoiled daughter of a wealthy aristocrat who couldn't possibly deserve him. From what little I knew of love, even I could see he was in need of advice.

"Perhaps," I said, "you should start by paying closer attention to her."

He looked startled, then he laughed. "It's not that. I've never met her. We're betrothed. She arrives tomorrow. I need a wedding gift, and I've searched all the shops in Saint Sebastien with no success. So I came here."

He'd never met her. *Very* interesting.

He watched me, an uneasy expression forming on his face.

"Do I know you?"

I could only wish. "I don't believe so."

This didn't seem to relieve him any. "You think I'm an idiot, don't you?"

I was astounded. "Me? Think you . . . ? I beg your pardon, I . . ."

"You're right, of course," he said, beginning to pace back and forth.

He needed calming. "Perhaps," I began, in a soothing voice, "it would be better to learn what she likes before buying her anything."

He cut me off. "How can a gift say 'Forever' for someone I've never met? It's madness!"

On this, we agreed. Feeling reckless, I decided to encourage this line of thought.

"Perhaps a better sentiment for your first gift to this lady would be, 'Good Luck.'"

Oh, Aunt would dice me to hash for that if she heard it.

He clamped his jaw shut, and an iron look crossed his face.

Oh, dear. "'Bonne chance,' as the French would say?"

"An expert on human relations, I see," he said, nodding. "I don't suppose you believe love could last forever."

I'd hurt him. I looked away, chagrined.

"You're mistaken," I said. "I do believe it could. But it would depend upon the lovers."

He folded his arms and watched me, forcing me to return his gaze. Oh, those eyes.

"And what kind of lovers must they be?" he asked.

The You-and-Me kind? I bit my lip. True ones? How naive that would sound.

His gaze burned me, but I couldn't break away from it.

I was spared from answering by the sound of Uncle's heavy footsteps coming down the stairs. The spell was broken. The gentleman looked away. I took a deep breath.

"Here comes the goldsmith, sir," I said, curtsying to

my young Adonis. "He can help you place a custom order for something you care to describe. He's most skillful."

Uncle rounded the doorpost and stood, scratching his head. He smiled his absentminded smile at me, then looked at the young man. He grabbed hold of the countertop and leaned against it as he lowered himself down to an arthritic half-kneel.

"Your Majesty," he said.

Chapter 2

Your *what?*" I said.

"Er," said my customer.

"Prince Gregor, we are honored," said Uncle. At least one of us was cogent.

I flopped down onto my knees, which made me disappear behind the counter. I considered crawling underneath and hiding on a shelf. I looked up to see the prince—*the prince!*—peering down over the counter's edge at me.

"You don't need to do that," he said.

"Do what?"

"Get down on your knees. Unless you are proposing marriage."

I scrambled to my feet. "As you wish." I dusted off my skirt. "You know best." Stupid response! Could I mortify myself any more?

He turned and doffed his hat to Uncle, who'd only just barely gotten back on his feet.

"I fear I must be going, sir," he said. "I haven't time for a special order. I need something sooner." His eyes glanced my way. "Your shop assistant shows great promise."

He was mocking me. I was ridiculous to him.

Then he bowed to me. "A pleasure. Might I ask your name?"

As God is my witness, I swear this is true: I couldn't think what it was. I felt as nameless as an unwanted baby.

"Lucinda, Your Highness," Uncle said.

The prince's eyes were unreadable. "Good day to you, Miss Lucinda."

"And to you," I called over the thunking of the door. I watched him dart away down the street until his coat was a blue smudge on my window. Hoped he'd heard me. Hoped he hadn't.

Uncle and I faced each other, dumbstruck.

"What would Aunt say?" I whispered.

He put a finger over his lips. I nodded. Aunt, probably in her bedroom dreaming of all the things Beryl's coins would someday buy, need never know that Crown Prince Gregor was in her shop.

Then Uncle's eyes twinkled. "Handsome, ain't he, Lucinda?"

I hid my face behind my hands. "Handsome" didn't even scratch the scratch.

Chapter 3

"The *what* was in my shop?" Aunt shrieked. "The WHAT?"

Uncle and I eyed each other. From where I knelt washing the floor, her neck seemed to swell like a bullfrog's.

"The Amaranth Witch, my good lady," said Father Julian, who had burst into the shop out of breath a moment before. Now he stood mopping his shiny face with a handkerchief, as if it were August and not December. "She who put a curse upon Queen Rosamund these many years ago, when the queen was with child for the first time. She's not aged a day since. The witch, I mean to say. Comes of being in league with Satan."

This didn't strike me as a powerful reason *not* to be in league with Satan.

The red drained from Aunt's face, leaving it the color of cheese curd. She gripped the edge of the countertop.

Nobody spoke for an awkward minute. A day of bewilderments, to be sure. Nothing like this ever happened at Montescue's Goldsmithy.

"But are you certain?" Her imploring eyes searched Father Julian's face.

He nodded, his jowls quivering. "I saw her leave your shop. She frequents the city, and must live nearby, but she's managed by her arts to remain concealed. I endeavored to follow her, but I"—he patted his chest feebly—"I succumbed to her trickery. One moment she was a few paces ahead of me, and the next"—he snapped his fingers—"she vanished."

Aunt crossed herself.

Losing someone on a city street was no great marvel. Pickpockets did it daily. But Father Julian nodded as if this were ominous news. "She led me to some part of the city I'd never seen before, and I doubt if I searched I'd find it again." He smoothed the strands of hair on his balding crown. "I came back to warn you," he said, bending forward, "against accepting the devil's gold."

It was hard to judge who looked more scandalized—Father Julian, who could act onstage if ever the Church grew tired of him; Aunt, whose boundless greed was matched only by witless superstitions; or Uncle, who wasn't avaricious, senseless, or pious, but who knew well how hard the mortgage money had come of late. I felt for him. Here at last was a customer, with worthy traffic and solid payment, and now we must turn her away?

"We haven't taken any of her gold," Uncle said.

"Oh, what should we do?" Aunt implored, as if she hadn't heard Uncle. She clasped both hands together atop her considerable bosom. "How do we cast this evil from us?"

"Turn away her business," the priest said. "Send back her accursed objects and have no more to do with her."

"What if she puts a curse on us?" Uncle asked. I watched him. The corner of his mouth twitched ever so slightly.

I knelt forgotten in a shadowy corner, trying to picture the woman Beryl as a dangerous witch. It seemed laughable. But then, if she was a sorceress, she'd be practiced at deceit. Witches wore many disguises. Still, someone that exquisite?

I decided I didn't believe Father Julian. A shocking lack of piety, no doubt, but then, Aunt rarely let me go to Mass, so if I'd grown into a heathen, it was no one's fault but hers.

Aunt, who hadn't stopped crossing herself, raised both hands in the air. "Enough!" she cried. She glared at Uncle, then reached for Father Julian's hands. "We shall send her away," she announced. "Though it cost us the roof over our heads and the bread in our mouths, we shall send her away."

Father Julian bowed low. "May God protect this establishment from the works of darkness." Avoiding Uncle's gaze, he left and disappeared down the street.

Uncle lumbered over to his workbench and sat down heavily. "Well, there it is," he said.

Aunt whirled to face him. "There it is, Husband, and I'll hear not another word about it. I'll have no traffic with the devil, not if we're down to our last speck of flour, and no more would you, if you had your proper feelings about you."

Uncle held a magnifying glass to study a broken pendant. *My* broken pendant.

Aunt stood fuming. She yanked the red leather book from its shelf. She opened it to the last page and scrutinized the writing. "That'd be a witch's hand, all right. Too fancy for an honest woman." As if she'd know.

She watched me, biting her lip, which she always did when scheming new punishments. Then she smiled, which was even more frightening.

"Lucinda," she said—she never used my name—"you'd like an outing, wouldn't you?"

I smelled treachery. From her pocket, she produced Beryl's luminous gem.

"Go to this address and return the jewel to the witch. Tell her your uncle is poorly, and he won't be able to do the job." With each sentence she nodded, as if explaining something to a simpleton. "Do you understand?"

For heaven's sake. I wasn't a baby.

"Yes, Aunt. I understand." I understand that just in case this witch puts a curse on the messenger returning her stone, you're sending me.

Aunt straightened up and reverted to her normal manner.

"Then get going!" She left the room.

Uncle looked over at me. I said nothing, but with my face I wordlessly begged him to reconsider. We needed the money. But he shook his head.

"Take it straight there, Lucinda," Uncle said. "We don't want a gem like that getting stolen."

The subject was closed.

I nodded. "Yes, sir."

Chapter 4

That night, after finishing the dishes, I climbed the ladder to my attic bedroom, sat down on my cot, kicked off my shoes, and did some hard thinking about Beryl's gemstone.

I hadn't returned it. I didn't search out Beryl's house, or even try. I left the shop repeating over and over to myself the address where Beryl lived, but I never went there. I meandered until supper. And I only thought of the prince two-thirds of the time.

It was ridiculous to return the stone! That was all I could figure. We needed the money desperately. I'd decided, out there on the gray streets of Saint Sebastien, that Uncle could forge a new setting in secret, and I could deliver it and collect the payment. Uncle could use the money as he saw fit, and for once he'd have control of some of the gold he'd earned.

I told Aunt I'd returned the stone. I decided to corner Uncle in the morning and explain my plan to him. He'd be worried about Aunt, I knew, but I was sure I could persuade him. For once, we might be able to have beef for Sunday dinner and enough coal for the fire. Beryl would get her gem, everyone would be happy, and Aunt, none the wiser.

I pulled the stone from my pocket and admired it by candlelight.

"What are you?" I asked it. "Milk made crystal? Child of pearl and diamond?"

It was no great stretch to imagine the gem could answer.

I'd carried it concealed in my pocket all afternoon, but now, lying in my palm, it shimmered with energy. It seemed lit from within, burning but never consumed. Perhaps that was only a trick of the candlelight. And so heavy! No wonder Beryl's former setting had broken.

I set it on the crate that served as my bedside table, and dressed for bed. I pulled my second dress over my first, and my good stockings over the everyday ones for warmth, lay down on the cot, blew out the candle, and pulled my thin blankets up to my chin. On a second thought, I reached for the stone and slid it into the pocket of my outer dress.

The sky was starless, covered with clouds threatening snow. I hoped so. Better snow than mud. Snow felt like Christmas, and Christmas, no matter how Aunt might spoil it, felt like Mama and Papa, and roasted goose trimmed with holly, salted nuts and candied cherries, and oranges and apples imported from the sun's winter home.

I rubbed my feet together and tried to remember being warm until I drifted off to sleep.

A scuttling noise overhead woke me. Rats on the roof. I squeezed my eyes shut.

The second thump was much too heavy for a rat. I sat up, half-asleep, half-terrified.

I went to the window, rubbing my eyes. A few lamps at street level gave a faint glimmer to the roof just below my dormer window. Its slate tiles were covered in frost.

My breath fogged up the window.

I jumped back as a dark face appeared, staring at me.

I clapped my hand over my mouth to stifle a scream. Never. Wake. Aunt. Ever.

The face came closer, and a ghostly looking hand rapped on the glass. "Let me in!"

I stared at the shadowy face. A boy. Older than me but not by much. His face was pinched with cold and panic.

Wait a minute. I knew that face. I'd seen him about town often enough. One of the city's many youths who loaf about with no apparent aim and no parents to tell them not to. Harmless, more or less, I'd have said, unlike some I knew of. Just the other day I'd seen him loitering around our shop. When I'd stuck my head out the door to ask him his business, he laughed and took off running in mismatched shoes.

Now he saw me and gestured frantically for me to open the window. "Let me in!"

I put a finger over my mouth and signaled him to be quiet. He only pounded louder. The wavy glass rattled in its frame.

"Stop it!" I hissed. "Don't be stupid! You'll get us both into big trouble!"

He crouched on the thin lip of roof. Nothing between him and a three-story drop. He slid his fingers all around the casement, trying to pry it up. I grabbed the handle and pulled down with all my weight.

I didn't weigh enough. In an instant he had the window open and tumbled inside. He pulled the window shut, then grabbed me by the shoulders.

"Don't touch me!" I yelped.

"Hide me!" he whispered.

I blinked. "Hide you?"

He shook me. "Are you deaf? I need a place to hide. Quick!" He let go and pawed around the garret.

Another noise sounded from the roof. Approaching footsteps. He flattened himself against the wall beside the window, and I did the same, craning my neck to see him. In the darkness I could just make out long, dark sheets of dirty hair, a dirty face, and a moth-eaten coat. What a contrast to the other young man I'd met today—

and the odds of me meeting young men, most days, were zero.

He cocked his head, listening hard to the ceiling.

The footsteps stopped close by. We stared at each other. His eyes were wide, and his finger flew over his lips. I nodded. My heart pounded as if I were the one being chased.

The footsteps moved toward the window.

"Back! Back!" he mouthed. I pressed myself farther into the shadows under the eaves.

What was I doing? Why was I helping him hide? I ought to scream, I knew, but I didn't. His eyes pleaded with me. From one penniless youth to another . . . I couldn't toss him to the wolves, be they the constables, his pursuer, or Aunt.

A shadow passed across the pale glimmer of light that came in through the window. It moved back and forth, snakelike, as if someone was searching for something.

I willed my breath to be silent and slow. But each exhale, each heartbeat felt blaring. Surely whoever was on the roof would hear. The boy closed his eyes as if to pray, and waited.

The shadow departed, the footsteps retracted then went silent. The boy in the shadows crept forward, motioning to me to remain quiet.

We waited for an eternity. Then, "Well," he said, cracking his knuckles, "that went well, don't you think?"

I jumped at the shattered silence, then shook myself. All my fear turned to indignation.

"Listen here!" I said, whispering as loud as I dared. "You can't just barge in here like this! I don't care what you're running from. If my aunt catches you, you'll be worse off than if . . . whoever *that* was did." I tiptoed to the stairs to see if Aunt and Uncle had slept through this ruckus.

"Good of you to keep quiet," he went on, as if he hadn't heard a word I said. "That's hard for girls. Don't get me wrong, I've got nothing against girls, but if there's one thing about them, it's noise."

He should talk about noise!

No sounds came from below except snores. True, Aunt went to bed with two brandies, and Uncle slept like the dead, but the footsteps and window banging could have wakened a mummy.

I turned back to my room. In the dark I could make out no sign of the boy.

"Where are you?"

Nothing.

He couldn't have left—not without my noticing. I groped around in the darkness, under a broken table, behind the old armoire, under the eaves. No sign of him.

"I know you're in here somewhere," I said. "If you don't show yourself, I'll stick my head out that window and scream until your friend comes running."

Silence. Then, "There's room."

I jumped. His voice came from close by, on my bed.

I recoiled in disgust. Thought he and I'd be cozy now, did he?

"There's room here beside me," came his voice again, sounding impatient. "It's warmer that way. Why don't you lie down?"

"Next to *you*? No, thank you! You've gotten my help, but if you think you're going to get a kiss out of me, you've got another thing coming."

"I'm not going to touch you." He sounded amused. "I just need a place to sleep. So you can either lie down or sleep standing up. It makes no difference to me." My bed creaked as he shifted in it.

I feared him about as much as I feared a moth, but I felt I needed to remind him that I, at least, had a sense of propriety. "How do I know you're trustworthy?"

"Gentleman's honor," he drawled.

"Gentleman indeed!"

Sanctuary was one thing, lodgings quite another. To rescue a soul in distress, yes; to give up my bed for a cocky ruffian, not tonight. I reached for my bed and felt him in it, his shoulder damp with rank cold sweat, cozying up under my blanket. Those blankets might not have been much, but they were mine, and clean. I grabbed his ear and twisted it. He squawked.

"I don't know who you're hiding from or why. You've put me at risk of a smacking, and it's going to cost you.

And you'll not have my bed, nor stink up my blankets, not for all your cheek, and I don't care who you are. You can sleep on the floor." I gave his ear another twist.

He swatted at my hand. "Git off! Not the floor. I won't!"

"Then hang from the ceiling with the bats," I said, "but get out of my bed, or I'll pluck out your eyes."

"I get this blanket, then," he said. "Some lady you are."

I snatched the blanket back. "There are some canvas bags in that corner. And I never claimed to be a lady." Though once I could have.

He gathered a handful of sacks and arranged them under a stream of curses.

"I suppose you're used to better?" I said, tucking myself back into bed. "Missing our silk sheets tonight, are we?"

"For your information," he said, "I've slept in some of the finest beds in Saint Sebastien. Even slept in the king's bed, once, at his country house."

"You have not, you liar."

"Have so."

"Does the king snore?"

"He wasn't in it, idiot," he said. "He wasn't at home at the time."

"How'd you get in, then?"

He was silent for a moment. Then, "I'm handy with a lock."

"Shouldn't wonder."

I listened to his breathing. It was odd to have someone

else in the room with me. For an instant I remembered sleeping in my infant nursery, with my nurse nearby.

"Who was after you?" I asked. "Let me guess: the king's constables."

"Pah. Not at this hour. And not on the rooftops!"

"Well? Who was it?"

A long pause. "A thief."

This made sense: some alleyway fisticuffs, flight up a ladder to evade his assailant, a mad dash across slippery roof tiles. It could have come right out of a novel. Boys had all the fun.

"Why was a thief chasing you?"

Floorboards creaked as he shifted around, looking for a better position. "Do you always talk this much, or just at night?" he said.

I chose not to answer his rudeness. He lay still, except for his gurgling stomach.

"You're hungry," I said.

"No. I just ate a stuffed pheasant, and I'm here for tea." He paused. "You got any bread?"

I smiled in the dark. "No. When did you eat last?"

He said nothing.

I chewed on my lower lip. "I can get you some early in the morning, if you promise to clear out after that." I took his grunt as a yes.

Warmth began to tingle and spread over me once more. Even with tonight's commotion, I could feel sleep claiming me. But there was one more thing I needed to know.

"What's your name?"

He snorted like he'd just been startled awake. "What?"

"Your name."

He slapped something—his forehead, I presumed—and groaned.

"What's the matter, are you sick?" I asked.

"Peter," he said. "It's Peter. All right?"

"It'll do," I said. "As names go. I myself might have chosen Edmond, or Roderick, but Peter will do well enough."

"Thank you."

"You're welcome."

"Hmph," he said.

"I'm Lucinda. Thank you for asking."

Chapter 5

I woke gradually, as always, fighting every inch of the way. There was never enough sleep. Especially when morning brought chores and chamber pots.

This morning I woke before Aunt's summons with a nagging thought I couldn't locate. Something I had to do today? Telling Uncle about the stone. Yes. That was it. I reached for my thigh and felt for the stone still in my dress pocket. All was well.

No, it wasn't just the stone. The boy! My wooden cot groaned as I bolted upright.

There he was, fast asleep on my floor, surrounded by canvas sacks. One arm was thrown over his face, and both great toes poked through large holes in his stocking feet. In the pale light of morning he looked much less the rogue hero of the streets that I'd imagined. In fact, he looked and smelled in desperate need of a bath.

Still, he had dropped out of the sky, more or less, into the dreariness of my life, and for that, I could pilfer breakfast for him. And after I fed him, he'd disappear.

I glanced out the window. No snow. The clouds misled me.

I hurried downstairs before Aunt could come up to rouse me. Usually she only yelled from the foot of the ladder, but there were times when she came up, just to keep things lively.

Other than a terse remark about the oddity of my getting myself up, Aunt said nothing at breakfast—particularly, to my relief, nothing at all about hearing strange noises in the night. Thank goodness for brandy nightcaps.

Uncle slept through breakfast. Aunt was tight-lipped and moody, and her eyes were red. I feared she may have a headache, which was bound to mean triple misery for me. It would be a long day. She was so distracted she didn't notice me slip my two slices of dry bread into my apron pocket. I made the excuse of needing to return to my room to straighten it up, and left the table, climbed the ladder to the garret, and poked my head through the trapdoor.

"Oh!"

Peter sat on my bed, wrapped in my blankets, fingering the things on my bedside crate. Trunks of Aunt's had been opened, their contents strewn about.

"Hullo," he said. "I suppose you've brought breakfast?"

I scrambled the rest of the way up and closed the trap-door gingerly.

"What are you doing?" I hissed. "What's the meaning of all this mess?"

"Easy, easy," he said. "No need to fuss. How about that breakfast?"

"Hush! My aunt's awake now." I folded my arms across my chest in my best Aunt imitation. It didn't seem to bother him. In the light of day I saw that what I'd mistaken for dirt on his face was a jagged mark down one cheek.

He held his hands out, then patted *my* bed beside him as if inviting me to sit down, the pompous donkey. His greasy, disheveled hair was tangled just like my bedding, curse him.

"We didn't get off on the best foot last night," he began. "I suppose I was abrupt." He took a big bite of bread, and I gasped, realizing he'd reached into my apron pocket and pulled the bread out without my noticing.

"Necessity," he went on, chewing largely, "will do that to you. You go through life, well meaning as a cricket, but sometimes you need to borrow a bit, to make things smooth. Like how I needed to borrow a bed from you last night. Which"—he pulled the other slice from my pocket; I slapped his wrist—"you lacked the Christian upbringing to share with me. But we'll overlook that. No, no . . ."

"Will you shut up?"

He held up a hand. "We'll attribute it to my bursting in upon you. It caught you off guard. Ordinarily I would have written first, or left a card. By the way," he said, waving his last crust of bread in my direction before devouring it, "a bit of butter wouldn't hurt, in the future."

I saw spots. "In . . . the . . . *future?*"

"Tomorrow, for instance," he said between bites. "Or the day after that. That's what we usually mean when we say 'future.'"

Insufferable peacock! "I know what it means! I took pity on you, and gave shelter to the poor, hungry, homeless boy, and you've gone and robbed me in return. 'Chased by a thief.' You're nothing but a thief yourself!"

"Stick with your first instincts, is a rule I live by," Peter said, nodding. "Take, for example, me. When I first saw you, polishing the windows of your warm shop, I said to myself, 'Now there's a place I might stay in comfort, and a lass who looks like she'd help me do it.' I followed that instinct, and see how right I was?"

He grinned, thoroughly pleased with himself, looking as though I should be too.

"You thought that, did you?" I hoisted the window upward. Coal smoke and cold hit my face. "Out, or I will call for the constables, and for Aunt, come what may. Now!"

"You won't call for anyone," he said, smug and self-assured, shoving his feet into his worn shoes. "But as a prior appointment beckons, it is time for me to be going."

He gripped the top of the window and slid his legs out, agile as a cat. On the ledge he turned and placed his hand on my cheek. "Farewell, sweet wench. Do not pine for me. Perhaps we shall meet again."

"Don't 'sweet wench' me! And get your filthy hands off!" I shoved at him. He started to topple backward.

I gasped. He caught himself, then shook his head at me.

"We shall overlook your carelessness this time. But you could have done us damage." He studied the back of his hand and his nails. "However, you are correct. Next time, a bath is in order. See to it. Adieu." He disappeared over the peak of the roof, as sure-footed as a squirrel.

I shut the window as quietly as I could and wiped my face with my sleeve. Then I got quickly to work straightening the garret before Aunt came to drag me downstairs.

Rude, impertinent, presumptuous, *filthy*! Who did he think he was? I'd give him a bath, all right, next time he passed by, with Aunt's chamber pot. Now there was a picture.

I heard the unmistakable stamp of Aunt's feet in the hall below. I whirled about, stuffing things back into their trunks and hiding what I couldn't stow underneath my cot. I shoved my hip against my bedside table crate to put it back into place.

Something was wrong. Missing. The jewel! I frisked myself, clutching at the folds of my skirt. Heaven help me.

The ladder's rungs squealed under Aunt's weight.

Hallelujah, there it was, heavy in my pocket still. I panted with relief.

I managed to appear to be straightening my bed when Aunt opened the trapdoor and stuck her head through.

"What's taking so long?"

I forced myself to slow my breathing.

"Nothing, Aunt."

She peered at me. "You've got a guilty look about you. Makes your face even plainer, if that's possible."

I looked at my toes. "Yes, Aunt."

Her eyes darted around the garret. I closed mine. Here it comes.

Silence.

Then, "You've got dishes and washing waiting downstairs. What have you been doing up here all this time?"

I opened my eyes. Aunt's cheeks were red from climbing the ladder, and her breath came in little puffs between words.

"Nothing," I said, looking at the floor. "I was straightening up. A rat knocked some things over in the night." How true.

"Leave off," she said. "I need you downstairs." Her head disappeared down the hole in the floor. Nine days out of ten I'd have gotten a beating for an untidy garret. I was so relieved I swayed in my boots.

If I ever laid eyes on that dratted Peter again, I swore I'd get my pound of flesh back from him for this.

Chapter 6

I pulled myself together and went down the ladder. Aunt met me at the kitchen door with the mop and bucket.

"I mopped yesterday," I said.

"Do it again."

My hands mopped the kitchen floor, my mind seethed at Peter's nerve. Perdition, the cat, yowled at me for sloshing his napping corner with suds.

When I'd finished the kitchen and hallways, I headed upstairs. I mopped the parlor, then reached for the door of Aunt and Uncle's bedroom. Aunt met me coming out.

"Leave this room be," she snapped. "Let your uncle rest."

I shrugged and carried the bucket back to the kitchen.

"Windows," Aunt said. "All of 'em."

"But I washed the windows yesterday morning," I said, then wished I hadn't.

Red spots appeared on Aunt's cheeks. "Windows."

"Yes, ma'am." I washed the windows.

It drew on toward nine o'clock, time for the shop to open, and still no sign of Uncle. Aunt passed out of their bedroom door and I thought she must be rousing him, but he didn't appear.

"Is Uncle unwell?" I asked when she passed through the parlor.

"Mind your business. When you're done there, polish the silver."

And then it was, "polish the woodwork in the shop and in the parlor." And then, "dust the china cabinets," and if I chipped so much as a saucer, she'd take it out of my backside. As if there was enough spare flesh on my backside to mend a chip. Not with what she fed me.

Where was Uncle? I needed to talk to him about the stone.

My belly growled a protest that I'd given up breakfast for such an unworthy as that blackguard Peter. But as the morning slipped away I forgot about Peter and worried more and more about Uncle and why he hadn't gotten up yet.

The shop remained closed, and passersby paused to wonder at the darkened windows. The sky was gray and heavy, though no snow fell. As I lifted and dusted each china curio, I imagined what might be wrong with Uncle, each thought more lurid than the next. A festering molar? Infectious fever? Typhus? Consumption?

The chores were done. I hung my rags in the kitchen corner and waited.

"Here, girl," Aunt called from down the hall. "You can come clean the bedroom now."

She stood at the door with mop, rags, and bucket.

"Is he awake?" I asked.

"Hmm." She opened the door.

Uncle lay on the bed, still sleeping, facing the opposite wall.

"Start with the windows," Aunt said. "Don't wake him." She shut the door behind her.

I tiptoed across the room and dipped a rag into the bucket. Drips fell and splashed into the suds. A clock ticked on the mantel.

Something was wrong. The hair on my neck stood on end. I turned around.

Uncle was resting peacefully, a small smile on his lips. I held my breath.

His breath never came.

I went to his side and touched his hand. It was cold.

Panic swept over me. I shook his shoulder and he barely budged. It felt like trying to roll a boulder. "No, no, no, no," I heard myself saying, as though I was watching myself from a corner of the room. "Uncle, please wake up. It's me, Lucinda."

Fear and shock tore me into two pieces. Part of me knew trying to wake him was in vain, the other part had to try. Lucinda watching from the corner couldn't persuade Lucinda by the bed that Uncle was plainly dead.

To act was better than to think. I ran to the door and yelled. "Aunt! Come quickly!"

I heard a kitchen chair creak and scrape against the floor, followed by her slow, heavy footsteps. My heart beat a dozen times between each of her steps. Why was she taking so long?

At last she appeared around the corner. "What is it?"

"It's Uncle," I said. "I think he's . . ." The dam broke, and I began to cry.

She pressed her lips together and pushed past me to the bed. She lifted Uncle's hand and listened at his nose and mouth. Then she straightened and looked at me.

I saw the charade in her eyes. She knew! She'd known since morning. She'd let me find him this way on purpose, but not until she'd gotten half a day's hard cleaning out of me.

She sucked on her lower lip, chewing it with her rodent teeth.

"Look what you've done to him," she said, her voice soft and deadly. "He's worn out from the burden of caring for you all these years, ever since your high-living parents died and left nothing provided for you. The strain killed him in the end. I hope you're pleased."

Aunt's red face and gray-clad body swam before my watery eyes. She always found new holes in my armor. Hateful lies and nonsense! Of course I didn't kill Uncle.

But maybe it was for my sake that he put up with her

so long. Maybe, if it weren't for me, he could have left the old shrew and found some gladness. Maybe she was right.

Aunt crossed the room and delivered a stinging slap to my face. "I'm just sorry he died before he could find out how you returned the thanks for all he's done for you, you thieving little vixen." She struck me on the other side, and this time, her hand was a fist.

This pain burned. I stumbled back out the door. "What?"

Aunt caught me, grabbed my chin and jerked it so I was forced to look at her. Her breath in my face was foul. "You have one minute to be gone from here, before I call the constables."

I tried to speak for myself. "Thieving? What—"

Aunt answered with her palm on my cheek. "Don't 'what?' me." *Slap.* "I've been to your room this morning." *Slap.* "Boxes of family heirlooms—" *Slap.* "Rifled through, precious ornaments and silver taken—the few things I have left of my poor mother's." *Slap.* "You've eaten your bread at our table your whole life, and this is how you thank us for our sweat and sacrifice." *Slap. Slap.*

The irony of it overwhelmed me. I'd endured her for Uncle's sake, and he'd endured her for mine. She trapped us both. And now, for Peter's theft and Uncle's death, I was blamed.

I stood tall. "I've never stolen anything from you, Aunt. I can explain about the missing things. There was a young man in my room last night, and he—"

Aunt screamed. "Taking up with men! A slattern, sneaking around with boys in her room while we sleep, bringing disgrace down on us!" She boxed both my ears. Then she reached for the poker by the stove and brandished it like a sword.

Had she gone mad? She had never used a weapon on me before, never done worse than what hands could do. Not with Uncle around.

I edged away.

She squinted, her stout bosom heaving, the end of her poker drawing circles in the air.

Then, looking shaken, she lowered it to the ground.

She held her index finger up before her nose. "One. Minute."

I swallowed and pushed past her toward the door. "I'll just go get my things."

She blocked my path with a meaty arm. "You have no things."

I turned and walked on shaky legs down the hall and through the shop. I felt as though someone was forcing me to walk off a cliff. What happens to a girl kicked out of her home and robbed of even her petty possessions?

I supposed I'd soon find out.

I let the door slam behind me.

Chapter 7

Freezing air drew me up sharp. My coat was one of the things I'd left behind.

Frost lay over the dingy shop windows of Feldspar Street like a coat of dust. I glanced up at Uncle's bedroom window.

"Good-bye, sir."

Then I hurried away before Aunt could decide to come outdoors and vent more of her spleen upon me. I stumbled around the corner, rubbing my hands together. My tears for Uncle froze upon my cheeks. Heaven reward him for his kindness to me, was all I could think. Perhaps he was with my parents now. And Evangeline, his first wife. I hoped wherever he was, there was roast pork and bread pudding aplenty.

I almost envied Uncle.

I walked for a while, thinking only of putting each foot

forward. When Aunt and the shop seemed truly behind me, I found a sheltered, abandoned doorway where I could sit and think. No use in just walking without making a plan.

I had no place to go, no person to go to. I couldn't stay out in the cold or I wouldn't survive the day.

Just yesterday seemed like a lifetime ago. Meeting the pretty prince and letting my fancy take hold of me. Meeting Peter, the rascal. Meeting the mysterious Beryl, and learning she was called, by some, the Amaranth Witch.

Yesterday I doubted the priest. Today I depended on him being wrong. Witch or no, if Beryl wanted a servant, she'd have one. In my pocket was my entrance ticket.

Her address was the Palisades, Riverside. Easy enough to remember. Almost as if I'd always known it.

The cold flagstones in the doorway chilled my backside right to the bones. I hugged my arms around myself and huddled into the smallest ball I could make.

The Palisades, Riverside. I was curious to get a glimpse of that place.

On the other hand . . .

The lady was nothing to me. Uncle would never know if I didn't return the stone. I could sell it for enough to live on in comfort for a long time.

Comfort. Something I hadn't known since I was five.

I didn't feel I owed Aunt any favors. It would serve her

right to have the woman come looking for her stone. Maybe, if she was a witch, she'd turn Aunt into a lizard. More likely, Aunt would blame me and haul me before the magistrate.

Aunt had accused me of being a thief. Did I want to prove her right?

I sat there confounded in the doorway until I noticed a light tugging on my hair.

A goat was eating it! A small brown billy had apparently ambled past me and decided to stop for lunch. He nibbled on the loose ends of my hair that spilled out from under my cap.

"Shoo! Go on!" I teased my hair from between his teeth and tried to scare him away. He looked at me out of one eye, like a rooster, and baaaahed.

"Where did you come from?"

He nibbled on my chin with rubbery lips.

I patted his coarse hair. A cloud of warmth hung around him, and I rubbed him with both hands to warm my fingers. He bleated, twisting his spine and backing up until his rear end was practically in my lap.

"What do you think you are, a dog?"

He butted me with his behind in reply and wagged his docked-off stump of a tail.

"Right then, Dog," I said, scratching between his stubby horns. "You're the strangest goat I ever did see."

The stone slab I sat on became unbearably cold, and

at last I rose and continued on my way up the main road, still unsure what to do. Dog fell into step at my heels, his hoofs clacking on the pavement. He baaahed and brayed at people we passed like he was announcing a passing dignitary.

The streets were full of people pouring in for the Winter Festival, which started in earnest the next day, but vendors came early to stake out the best spots. Even the royal family came and joined the party at festival time. All the city went wild, eating and drinking and spending to celebrate the winter solstice.

Dog and I pressed on. I wondered if he'd go back to where he'd come from. But he just butted my legs along when I paused.

I made my way in the direction of the bridge that would lead me to Riverside.

Was that it, then? Had I made my decision to go to the Palisades and return the jewel?

Better to cast myself at this woman's mercy than to freeze to death or be trampled underfoot at Winter Festival. Wasn't it?

Dog and I trotted on until we came to a wide intersection. Two streets, St. Honoré and Jericho, flowed into each other, creating swirling eddies of people and animals and carts, the wares in which bobbed on the surface like the debris from a shipwreck. A shepherd steering a flock of two dozen dark sheep created no small commotion as he corralled his charges through traffic. Passersby jeered, but he ignored them, murmuring to his agitated sheep from underneath his wide-brimmed hat.

Young ladies dressed as housemaids hurried along in twos and threes, pretending to ignore whistles from lanky youths in laborers' garb. A shiny coach pulled by a smart pair of matched bays tried to gain headway, its driver shouting at everyone to clear away, while a lady in the carriage rapped at the glass with her white-gloved knuckles.

I held on tight to one of Dog's horns and stepped off the curb into the fracas. We wound our way through the clot of sheep. Dog had plenty to say to them. The craggy-browed shepherd eyed me and said, in a deep voice, "He shall separate the sheep from the goats."

"Yessir." A Calvinist. I kept my head down and pressed forward. I was far from pious, but even I knew to keep my distance from fanatics.

At last we reached the other side, where Dog found a watering trough. I was so thirsty I could have dunked my head in alongside him. I cupped my hand under the trickle that fed the trough and drank.

The sun was past its highest point in the gray December sky, and its limp light reminded me of how hungry and tired I was. No breakfast, no lunch, no Uncle, no home. A heavy morning.

We crossed the bridge. I tried not to look down at the surging gray water below, edged with chunks of ice. Once across, I followed the road northward. Soon the commercial riverfront was far behind me, and gardens and fields replaced stores and buildings. Dog tore up mouthfuls of grass, which still lay thick and green despite several frosts. The farther I went, the grander each house became. All was calm here, the noises of the city dampened by distance. Rows of stately trees stood as leafless sentries.

A strange feeling came over me. I'd never heard such quiet. Serenity lay thick upon the lawns and gardens, the sculpted shrubbery and the marble statues. I couldn't understand why I felt so unsettled, at once both peaceful almost to the point of sleepiness, and agitated as though a mosquito was buzzing in my ear.

I rounded a curve in the road, and the thought came to me that around the bend I would see a marble archway. Four steps later, the archway came into view.

I froze. Dog butted me.

There was the arch I knew I'd see. How had I known? And why was it not quite right?

Ivy grew over it, taller than it ought to be. Thicker.

I took a step closer and faced the arch head-on. Carved in Roman letters across the top were the words, "The Palisades." The witch-woman's home.

Maybe, I reasoned, I could see it in my mind's eye because she was a witch, and there was some magic at play. If so, all the more reason to get rid of the gem and quit this place. Never mind employment.

I patted my pocket once again to be sure the stone was there, then took a slow step forward through the arch and up the drive. Every bush, every tree seemed familiar somehow, as though I'd seen them in a dream. Everything about the grounds was gracious and lovely, but familiar, too, a bittersweet familiarity shot with pain.

The house appeared once I'd rounded a corner through a grove of trees. It stood at a distance, partly obscured from view by the trees and a rise of ground. It seemed larger and grander than the king's palace in the center of the city. But for such a vast house, it was as lifeless as the grave. No servants worked on the grounds, no horses ran in the paddocks, and no smoke rose from its many chimneys. The windows gave no sign of light or movement within. But surely this was the address Beryl had given.

Somehow my feet carried me forward to the steps leading up to the door, and somehow Dog and I climbed them. My chest felt heavy and my head buzzed with confusion. I reached for the bell-pull and yanked it.

From behind the carved mahogany door chimes rang out, a snippet of the melody of one of Laurenz's patriotic songs. Each note rang clear and true, just as I had known it would.

Because it was my house.

◆　◆　◆

I sank to my knees and looked at my trembling hands, my rough gray dress, my dismal fingernails. I was dirtier than the granite masonry on which I knelt. Yet by rights it ought to have been mine.

Piecemeal memories came to me, of Papa playing, hiding behind the pillars and peeking out at me, of Mama reclining in a lounge chair and sipping lemonade, my puppy at her feet.

Dog nudged me, and I realized that footsteps were coming from inside. I stood and wiped my cheeks with the back of my hand, shoved some wayward hair back under my cap, and I braced myself for the opening door.

It *was* the woman from the shop. There was no mistaking her pale skin and paler hair, neither young nor old. I felt breathless, as if the air had grown thinner.

She was tall and slender, dressed in a plain gray gown that fell in a single drape from her shoulders to the ground. She wore no other ornament.

"Good day, Miss Chapdelaine," she said. "What have you done with my stone?"

I took a step back. I'd never told her my name. Hardly anyone knew it, in fact. Most people assumed I was a Montescue.

"I haven't done anything with it," I stammered. "I shouldn't have come." I backed away, almost falling over Dog.

The woman's eyes never left mine. "Why not? Why shouldn't you come to your childhood home?"

Not that I had needed confirmation, but when it came it hit me like a sack of flour swung at my stomach. The corners of my vision grew blurry, and I held on to a porch pillar for support. I felt lightheaded and stupid, as if I were burning with fever.

"I didn't know about the house," I said. "I only came here to bring you your stone, and because you'd said you wanted . . ." I closed my eyes. "Because my uncle didn't . . ." What to say? Did it matter anymore? "And anyway, now he can't. He's dead."

"I am sorry."

I looked up. I believed her.

"You were sent back because I am the Amaranth Witch, is that not right?"

I tried to swallow. "Then you are?"

She said nothing.

"A priest told us you were. I didn't believe it."

The corners of her lips rose slightly.

"But if you're not a witch, how do you know my name? And about the house?"

My tongue was fat and sticky. It was an effort to speak.

The woman spoke. "I know about you."

I blinked. My eyes ached.

"You do? Oh." I didn't have the strength to argue anything. I pressed my face against the cool marble pillar. Its solid density reassured me. It was the only thing around me that seemed to hold still. All I could think of was escape from this oppressive bewilderment. "Sorry to trouble you. I'll get along now." I told my body to let go of the pillar, but it wouldn't. I didn't know if my legs would hold me up, or if my mind would work at all.

"Please stop it," I said.

"Stop what?"

"Stop whatever you're doing to me."

"I'm not doing anything to you."

The white marble reminded me of the reason I'd come. I reached into my pocket.

"I brought you your stone," I said, holding out my hand.

She glanced at my hand then back at me. I looked at my open palm, where a dull gray river pebble lay.

My mind groped for any explanation. For a moment I thought that my dirtiness had gotten on the jewel, too, and I tried rubbing it with my sleeve to get the gray off.

The pale woman watched me. I feared I would vomit. I tried to think, but my mind was useless. The pebble seemed to be the only thing that wasn't quivering.

I dropped it on the patio floor. A little note rang out.

I thought of all I'd endured to get it here, and my hopes that Beryl would make me her servant and give me a home, whereas now I'd as much as confessed to a theft.

I wasn't a thief.

"Peter," I croaked.

The woman stepped quickly toward me, and I flinched, waiting for the blow to strike. She didn't hit me, but pried my fingers off the pillar with hands of steel.

Fear enveloped me. Without the pillar I felt naked. I fell back, and darkness closed in.

Chapter 8

Papa and Mama and I were dancing, round and round in the ballroom. I arched my back and let Papa's strong arms carry me, while overhead the gilt chandelier spun. When I pulled my body back upright, I felt my hair flying and saw faces and candles careening in a giant circle. I leaned close to Papa, and he held me tight.

"You're making her sick, August," Mama said.

"I'm not sick either," I said to Papa's waistcoat. I felt his laugh rumble through me.

"I have the prettiest dance partners in all of Laurenz," he said. "Don't I, Your Highness?"

"Indeed," boomed a stout man in glittering clothes, whose fingers twirled one end of his long mustache. "And that girl of yours, egad. Voice of an angel."

"But she's no angel when it's time for bed, are you?" Papa held me up so high in the air that I could have stepped on his cravat. "Here's Greta Mary, come to take you off to sleep."

"No, Papa, no! One more dance. I want to dance with the king!"

Both men laughed. Mama smiled. Her soft brown hair framed her face so beautifully that it made me ache. In her blue gown she was lovelier than the china doll that sat in my nursery.

Greta Mary, my nurse, appeared and curtsyed. Papa set me down, but I wouldn't acknowledge his "Good night, Lucinda."

The stout man bent low and whispered in my ear, loud enough for my parents to hear. "When your parents present you, little Miss Chapdelaine, you shall have a dance with the king, and two dances with the prince. All right?"

I looked in the direction the man pointed, to where a little boy in red stockings and a blue velvet coat sat with a glass of punch in each hand and a cherry-colored stain around his mouth.

I wrinkled my nose. "I don't want to dance with *him*."

Greta Mary swooped down to shush me. A tall man in a black suit with tails that nearly reached the floor appeared at Papa's side and tapped his shoulder.

Papa turned and laughed, elbowing the king. "Look, it's William Coxley, tiptoeing like a priest, startling the daylights out of me. What is it, man?"

William Coxley said something to my papa in a deep voice, using words I couldn't understand, something about papers in the library. Greta Mary, who never lingered when Papa discussed business, lunged for my hand, but I clung tight to Papa.

"What, now?" Papa's eyebrows rose. "In the middle of a party? Surely it can wait till morning."

The man's mouth was a line even when speaking. "Very good, Mr. Chapdelaine."

Papa waved his hand. "Over there, Coxley, are two of Lady Huxtable's daughters. Lovely girls without a partner. Why don't you take your pick and invite one of them to dance?"

The tall man made a curt reply that I couldn't make out, bowed mechanically, and stalked off in the other direction, away from the Huxtable ladies.

Greta Mary, her face flushed red, tugged on my hand. "Come along, Miss Lucinda. Say your good-byes and come like a good girl."

"But I don't want to go to bed!"

Mama kissed me. "Go quietly, and I'll come up and see you before you go to sleep."

"Promise?"

"I promise."

"Good night, Papa. Good night, Mama. Good night, sir."

The crowd of finely dressed adults parted before us, and Greta Mary led me up the stairs. She helped me out of my party clothes and into a nightgown, and tucked me into bed.

My blankets and pillows enveloped me in softness. My puppy jumped up on the foot of my bed and warmed my toes. Greta Mary sat in her rocker by the fire and began to knit. The creak of the rockers and the dance of firelight on the ceiling overcame me, and I was asleep long before Mama came to say good night.

Chapter 9

It was still dark when I awoke. The fire had burned down to red cinders, throwing a red glow upon Greta Mary's chair.

I sat up. "Has Mama come?"

There was no one in the chair. Confusion came over me. I reached out a hand, grasping at darkness.

I was in my old bedroom, that much was certain. But Greta Mary wasn't here, and I was fifteen, not five, and Mama and Papa weren't downstairs dancing. They slumbered in the burial ground.

Finally I sat up and threw back the covers. My feet hit the cold floor, and all the blood drained from my belly. It prickled in my feet, making me lame. I hobbled toward the fire and saw that a small pot sat in the embers, emitting a delicious fragrance.

There was a rag nearby, and I used it to clutch the lid

and lift it off the pot. Soup. And on a small table by the foot of my bed, a clean setting of dishes.

Stories of witches poisoning young girls came to mind, but I dismissed them. In the stories, the witches were ugly hags with warty faces, and the girls were beautiful princesses. Hence, I was safe. Not very sound reasoning, but it reassured me.

The soup was bland and slightly bitter with flecks of dried herbs. It was perfect. I set down my bowl and heard Dog bleating outside. It comforted me mightily.

I laced on my shoes, which stood at attention nearby.

Beryl.

Why had she brought me to my bedroom and fed me?

Why hadn't she beaten me or at least scolded me?

Who was she?

I didn't know if I was a prisoner in her home, or a guest, but I decided to go find her and ask. I had a sense of where she'd be. I opened the door and stepped into the dark hallway.

I found the door I wanted and opened it. My foot reached for the stairs, overestimating their height. Of course. I was bigger now. I adjusted my steps and climbed the winding staircase to the many-windowed room at the top of the house. The tower room, where Papa used to sit at night and watch through his spyglass for the lights of his ships returning from across the sea.

She sat in a cushioned chair in the middle of the room.

There was no candle or fire, but reflected moonlight threw a pale glow over empty flowerpots, damask chairs, and the mounted telescope, looking like a long-legged hunchback draped in a cloak of dusty leather. A pane of glass was missing from more than one window, and night noises climbed inside.

I sat in a chair opposite Beryl.

"Why do you live in my home?" I asked.

"What have you done with my stone?" was her answer.

A swell of anxiety rose in my throat.

"Are you a witch?"

"Are you a thief?"

Now I was angry.

"If I was a thief, why would I have come back here to confess and prove it to you?" I demanded.

"If I was a witch, why wouldn't I have killed you by now? Or cursed you with warts?"

My hands flew up to my face. It was still smooth, though tender where Aunt had struck me. I chided myself for checking.

We were at an impasse. I could think of nothing else to say. I debated rising to my feet to see if I could walk out as easily as I'd walked in. I had just decided to try it when she spoke.

"I bought this house. Years ago. From a lawyer who was selling it. The owners had died in an accident."

In the dim light I felt safe when my eyes grew wet. It

had been so long since I'd last heard them mentioned. I needed a change of subject.

"What is an amaranth?"

She smiled faintly. "A mythical flower that never dies. There's also a real flower called by that name. I have several of them growing here in pots. I'll show you. Another name for it is 'Love-lies-bleeding.'"

I studied Beryl's face as she studied mine.

"Beryl. That's not your true name, is it?" She said nothing. I tried another angle. "How did you know my name?"

She laughed a little. "I know many things, but that took no . . . *magic,* as you might want to call it." She smiled a wry smile. "You're the exact image of your mother. There are several paintings of her here."

It was all I could do not to jump up and go searching for them. They'd be easier to see in the morning, I told myself.

"I'd heard about a daughter who was sent to live with relatives," she went on. "I often wondered what became of her. When I saw you in the shop, I was pretty sure I'd found my answer. When you showed up at my door, I was certain."

How could a painting of Mama tell her who I was? I didn't look much like Mama, so far as I could tell.

"You didn't look happy there," she said.

This puzzled me. "Is that why you spoke for me? Because you pitied me?"

She watched me for a moment. I became conscious of

the wind whistling through the open windows, and a night bird calling off in the trees beyond the lawns.

"What is your given name?" she asked softly.

It seemed as though I was bound to never get a straight answer from her. Yet something made me trust her, made me willing to reveal my name.

"Lucinda," I said.

"*Should* I pity you, Lucinda?" she asked.

I sat very still, feeling pricked by her question. Perhaps I pitied myself, but I didn't need her to.

"No."

She nodded her head, as if my answer pleased her.

"And yet," she said, "you have bruises on your face that weren't there yesterday."

I hadn't known they showed.

"Was it your aunt?"

There was no need to answer.

I was startled to see the great sadness written on her face. She rose from her chair and approached mine.

"May I?" she said. She knelt before me and slowly placed her hands over my eyes and cheeks. Her hands were cool, the skin taut and fine over hard muscles and bones. At her touch, the wounds stung and burned, until a sweet numbness came over them. She pressed more firmly, then removed her hands.

My breath came fast and heavy. I patted my face. It was warm, no longer numb or hurt.

"Are the bruises gone?" I asked.

She nodded.

I couldn't believe what had just happened. Who *was* she? "Thank you," I said, not without some fear.

"You are welcome."

"Is this why they call you Amaranth?" I said. "You can heal yourself, so you don't seem to get older?"

She smiled. "I chose the name, actually. It seemed to fit. I loved the flower because it reminded me of home. I called myself 'Amaranth' in a town where I lived for a time, and the name stuck when I traveled here."

I tried to gather together the things I knew, or thought I knew, about her. What else had Father Julian said? "Did you really curse the queen when she was expecting a child?"

She sagged in her chair. "The only person I've ever cursed is myself. No," she said suddenly, "I must amend that. There are two others. But neither of them was the queen. She was simply unlucky."

I sat, wondering how she could have cursed herself. Her words interrupted my thoughts.

"I told your aunt that I was looking for a servant," Beryl said, "but that was not quite true. I am looking for help of a different kind, and when I saw you, I felt you could be just the person I needed." She stroked her fingertips across her collarbone, as if searching for something that wasn't there.

"I don't know how I could help you, unless you want your floors scrubbed. You're . . . well, if you're not a witch, you're something. There's nothing I could do that you could not."

She sat silently. I waited for her to say something. I'd nearly given up when she spoke.

"Do you know what it's like to be alone, Lucinda?"

This question wasn't what I'd been expecting. It made me stop and consider.

"I've been alone since my parents died, mostly," I said. "Uncle was good to me, but Aunt made it hard for both of us. I've never had friends to speak of."

She leaned forward in her chair, gripping the armrests. "That makes two of us, utterly alone, doesn't it?"

The wind pouring through broken windowpanes blew cold over my skin. "I suppose it does."

"What would you give to have a friend? One true friend, who would never leave you?"

"I suppose I'd give a lot for that." My mouth felt dry, parched. I wanted to end this interview. "You said there was something you needed from me?"

A flicker of disappointment crossed her face, then it was gone. "Yes. Well." She folded her hands in her lap and sat more erect, businesslike. "Where is my stone?"

Hope sank like a stone in my stomach. I had hoped that maybe the subject wouldn't come up again. "I don't know."

Outside on the lawn, Dog bleated. Beryl rose from her chair and stood at the window, looking down on the grounds. Moonlight on her pale features turned her into a marble sculpture. She kept her eyes fixed on some faraway sight—perhaps the sea.

I joined her at the window, drawn by curiosity. Saint Sebastien sparkled like a field of stars, and beyond it lay the deep black of the ocean.

"Who is this Peter that you mentioned?"

"I hardly know him," I said. I told her the story of how Peter came bursting into the room, spent the night, and disappeared, leaving a pebble in my pocket. Beryl listened intently, frowning more and more as I went on.

She seized my arm. "Lucinda," she said, when I was finished, "the day you wandered about the city, when your aunt and uncle had asked you to return the stone, but you didn't"—I felt my cheeks getting red—"did anyone approach you, or talk to you, or any such thing?"

I thought I knew where she was headed—that perhaps the stone had been stolen before Peter came.

"No," I said, "not a soul. And anyway, I had the stone in my room that night. I remember looking at it. It almost felt . . . alive."

Beryl clenched and unclenched her fists, growing more agitated by the minute.

"It doesn't seem as if . . . it doesn't sound like . . . could it be?" She was talking to herself now.

"Could it be *what*?"

Her eyes met mine. "Twice, in the city, someone has tried to steal the stone from me," she said. "A man. That's how the setting broke. I took it for repair in part to put it beyond the thief's reach. But I don't know who the thief is."

I began to see the cause of her fear. "You think Peter was working for someone else?"

She pressed her lips together tightly. "I hope not."

I searched back in my mind, thinking of the night he came. "I'm sure it isn't so," I said. But whether it was or no, what could *I* do about it?

Beryl began pacing the floor. "We don't know for certain that Peter took it, but it seems the most probable," she said. "And we don't know where he is, or how to find him, but we know he frequents the city streets, yes?"

I nodded.

"And he's likely to be out and about during the Winter Festival, would you say?"

I nodded again.

"Do you think you could find him and get it back from him?"

I laughed. "Not a chance! He's as slippery as a tadpole!"

Beryl leaned forward once more, her violet eyes seeming to have a light of their own.

"What if," she said, biting off each word deliberately. "What if I gave you something in return?"

She had my attention. But still, there was no way I could get the stone back from Peter.

"What if I gave you this house in return for my jewel?"

A cold breeze from the window blew over me, but I was already frozen with shock.

My house?

My house?

It was impossible!

My chances were miniscule at best.

Yet, the fact that there was a chance at all was irresistible.

She watched my face closely, apparently concerned that I hadn't answered yet.

"And," she added, as if to sweeten the deal, "all the gold you'll ever need to live here comfortably for the rest of your life."

I laughed out loud. The absurdity of it all was too much. She thought the first offer wasn't good enough for me? What else might I throw into this bargain—a royal crown?

"Where did you get such wealth? And what in heaven's name is this stone of yours?" I asked. "It's rare, I know, and huge, and priceless, even I can see that. But how could it be worth so much to you?"

A cloud passed over the moon, leaving us standing in darkness. I couldn't see Beryl at all, nor even hear her breathing. For an odd instant, I imagined she was no longer there—that she was a ghost or a vision who had vanished.

Then she spoke.

"Would you believe me if I told you that the stone is . . . how shall I describe this, the words are so shallow . . . that the stone is my *soul*?"

I heard my heartbeat thrum in my ears. What could I say to that? "I am listening."

"Yes," she said bitterly, "I know you are. But you're not believing."

Was I not?

"I am trying to," I said. "It's much to believe."

The clouds passed before the moon, and Beryl appeared again, ghostlike. Her arms were wrapped tightly around her body, as if it took all her strength to hold herself together in one piece. One fist she pressed into her lips and chin as if she were trying to knead away a toothache.

"I've said too much already," she said miserably. "You couldn't possibly understand, much less believe me."

I reached forward and touched her arm. She was cold and hard, yet pulsing with life, just like her stone had been. The feel of her skin unnerved me. She jumped a little at my touch, and met my gaze. I pulled my hand back.

"Who *are* you?" I said.

"Do you mean, what am I?"

I nodded. "I suppose I do."

She looked back out over the sea. "I am someone very lonely."

I reached out again, and this time I didn't flinch. "You

can trust me, Beryl," I said. "I won't hurt you." I took a deep breath. "And I'll try to believe."

She gripped my hand so tightly, I had to stifle a squeak. She looked down at my hand, held in hers.

"You're cold. Come downstairs. We can build a fire, and I will try to tell you."

Chapter 10

We sat by the fireplace in the drawing room. Beryl lit a fire from the dusty logs in the grate while I threw back the canvas drapes that covered the nearest couch. I sat on one end, watching as she lit the tapers on a pair of candelabra and set them on the mantel.

The walls were covered in paintings, from the chair rail up to the ceiling. A few were portraits of my family, but the rest were different, in a style like nothing I'd ever seen. The colors were intense, deep reds and blues, plays of dark and light in stark contrast, and the people in the paintings were not sitting still for portraits, but doing things—throwing javelins, tossing laughing children in the air, stroking animals, gathering fruit. I had never seen such lifelike paintings. No, that was not correct. Those people weren't *life*like. They were more alive than life.

They were people like Beryl.

Over the mantel was a painting I did not recognize. I approached to study it. A reclining figure sat by a stream, surrounded by luxuriant blossoms of purplish red. His smiling face was the picture of youthful beauty and vitality. It struck my heart. I turned and sat on the couch.

Beryl sat on the other end of the couch and looked at her hands in her lap. Dog, whom I'd insisted should come in, sat on my feet and chewed the canvas drape that lay on the floor.

The fire crackled. Candlelight wavered on the walls, where gilding on the plaster scrollwork had begun to peel. How Mama would feel to see the cobwebs, I hated to think.

Beryl seemed lost in thought. Her face, so pale in the moonlight, now took on the amber color of firelight.

"What was it you wanted to tell me?" I ventured at last.

Beryl nodded, as if resigning herself to what she was about to say, despite her better judgment.

"To tell you who I am, I must tell you about the place I come from." She smiled. "It's probably no surprise to you to hear me say that I am not from the kingdom of Laurenz, nor any place near here."

No surprise, indeed. That was a bit of an understatement.

"Do you believe in heaven?"

I blinked. "Are you saying you came here from *heaven?*"

Beryl looked alarmed.

"Certainly not. I'm trying to figure out your beliefs, your thoughts about . . . this world, and . . . other places besides this world. Like heaven. But not heaven."

"You're confusing me."

"I'm sorry. It's . . . let me try it this way. You live on this earth, you watch your sun rise and set, you see your moon at night, and all the stars."

I nodded.

"I come from a place that isn't part of this earth. Our sky holds a different sun and moons and stars."

A different sun? *Moons?* I tried to push my mind past that. I had promised to listen and try to believe.

Beryl watched my face anxiously.

"Go on," I said.

She seemed relieved, and she plunged on. "Perhaps it's wrong of me to tell you much. Perhaps it's unfair. Perhaps if I tell you about my home, I will be responsible for burdening you . . . for infecting you with my own misery. But how else can I explain?" She worried a silk handkerchief with her hands. It tore like old paper.

She saw the shreds in her lap and sighed.

"If I had my stone, I could show you." She looked up, a new hope in her eyes. "Can we find it first, and then I can show you everything?"

I looked at her, bewildered and unsatisfied.

"Please?" she said, almost timidly.

I looked over at the wall of paintings and saw one of

a little girl with thick dark curls tumbling helter-skelter around her face. She was wearing a pauper's dress, and kneeling on the ground in a forest. All around her was the beauty of a forest in spring, with dewy violets and snow-drops blossoming at her knees, but her face was fixed in a mask of despair. Quite a contrast from the smiling youth beside the stream. And yet, there was something similar in their faces.

"Did you paint these pictures?" I asked.

"All except the ones your mother painted," Beryl said.

I kept my face trained toward the wall. "Can't you tell me anything about the stone?"

Dog stood up and stretched, then leaned back on his haunches and placed both his hooves on my lap. He cocked his head to one side and peered at me through one of his devil's eyes. If goats could talk, I'd feel sure this one wanted to.

"It has tremendous power," Beryl said. "Without it I'm a shadow of myself."

I pondered this and stroked Dog's nose.

"How so?" I asked. "What does it do?"

She shook her head. "The stone, by itself, does nothing. It magnifies the soul of the bearer. Whatever seeds they have in themselves, the stone grows the fruit. It helps the mind open doors to the past, to other worlds, to souls themselves. It gives the bearer a clearer understanding, a fuller memory. If they are capable of happiness, the stone brings them joy."

I thought of the statues that guard the churches in the city, the stone carvings of glorious beings that are said to move as lightning and speak as thunder. It wasn't hard to picture Beryl's marble form among them.

"It turns you into an angel," I said.

She blinked, startled, as if seeing me for the first time. Then she sighed and shook her head bitterly. "If so, then, a fallen angel now."

She looked away.

"Will you ever grow old and feeble?"

"No."

"Will you ever die?"

"No."

I felt a thrill of fear prickle across my whole body. Someone who would never die. I shouldn't believe her, but I did.

Dog clambered into my lap.

"Such a doggy," I scolded, scratching behind his ears.

I looked back at Beryl. She was watching Dog with an odd, curious expression.

"Why are you here, Beryl, if this isn't the world where you belong?"

She seemed to search for an answer, gathering words gradually.

"Others have come before. Banished from my world, some have arrived here as a punishment. I wasn't banished. I came when I was very young. It was an accident, though I'm not without blame."

I couldn't see this flawless, ageless person carrying such a thing as blame. There she sat, looking more regal and graceful than any queen I could imagine—good heavens, just picture fat and jolly Queen Rosamond, for instance—how could it be? Blame was for the rest of us. Not someone like Beryl.

"How does one travel from your world to mine?"

She smiled for a moment. "You will think I'm joking."

I urged her on. "No, I won't."

She gave up. "Down a well."

"Down a *well?*" Evidently I'd lied. She *must* be joking.

She laughed faintly. "In your world, you have prisons for your little crimes, and gallows for your great ones. In our world, little crimes are few, and great ones almost none, but when they do happen, we would not kill the guilty even if we could. We send them away. Banish them. There is a well in my world, in the shadow of a mountain. When someone goes down that well, they travel to some other world—I believe not always the same one."

I was transfixed by her words. "And?"

She shook her head wearily. "And, I was curious about it. In the past, whenever anyone was banished—and it's so rare, Lucinda, so rare!—they go unwillingly, so it takes another to go with them, to force them down the well, making sure their banishment succeeds. It means that one member of the community must sacrifice themselves for the sake of the rest. It's horrible." She rested her face in her hands, as if she couldn't face herself. "Yet I went down the well myself. Stone and all. I wasn't planning to, at first. I just wanted to take a look. But I looked down the well, and I could hear sounds, great noises from far away, like the noises of many worlds rolling through space together. They called to me. I jumped in. And here I am."

I didn't know what to say. I wrapped my arms around Dog's neck and squeezed him. He lovingly ate my hair in return.

"I was a little girl, Lucinda. I'd been out filling my pockets with colorful pebbles from the stream. I followed the stream until it reached the valley of the stones and the well. I was so small, I crawled underneath the fence that guarded the well."

I watched the fire smolder down, felt the waves of heat it threw my way, red heat pulsing through the black embers. Was our world really such a prison? We had comforting fires and warm lap goats.

"Can't you go back?" I asked.

Her long lashes grew wet. "Not anymore."

"Because you were wrong to come?" I asked. She said nothing. "Because you don't have your stone?"

She pressed her lips tightly. "I would need it, yes, but that's not the reason, or I'd have gone back long since." She shook her head. "I can't go back because I'm guilty. They would strip me of my stone and banish me. So I remain here, banishing myself, but at least I've had the comfort of my stone."

I frowned. "What makes you guilty?"

She looked down at her hands, lying limp in her lap. She wouldn't meet my gaze.

"Murder."

Chapter 11

Dog rose from my lap and jumped down to the floor. He sat behind a covered chair, as if he'd had enough of the fire's heat, and started eating the drape that covered it.

I felt my hands grow trembly. Murder. I was sleeping alone under the roof of a murderer.

I was about to enter into an impossible bargain with a murderer.

There wasn't a living soul who knew I was here, or who cared. No one would come searching or wonder why Lucinda Chapdelaine had vanished.

Oh, Uncle, why did you have to die?

I wiped away the tears from my eyes and tried to put on a brave face. I looked up boldly at Beryl and saw tears streaming down her cheeks.

I wouldn't have thought a creature like her could cry.

"You hate me now," she said.

I said nothing.

"You fear me."

I rocked back and forth a bit on my hips, trying to wake up my resting body, in case I needed to spring up and try to get away.

"I can't blame you for hating me."

She seized my hands once more and I tried to pull away, but my wrists might as well have been enclosed in iron. She looked down at her hands holding mine and seemed to realize what she was doing. She let go.

"Don't go, Lucinda. I'm not a murderer. Please believe me."

I couldn't think what to do, so I stayed to listen. My senses were numb, my ears ringing. She searched my face and took courage from the fact that I wasn't leaving.

"I was a little girl," she said, her words tumbling out in a rush. "I came here as a child, something like ten years old in your years. I came here, and your earth races around its sun so quickly! Time sped for me. I aged quickly. Almost overnight, I was a young woman."

Earth races . . . sun . . . what?

I didn't have time for a lesson in physics.

"I fell in love," she said miserably. "Desperately in love with a young man in the village near where I'd . . . arrived. I had allowed a widow woman to take me in, and I helped her with housework. It saved me from people asking questions, or worse. But, as I said, I fell in love with this young man. He loved me, too."

I watched Beryl's face. Not even she could keep her marble composure in telling about this young man. Her eyes drifted toward the portrait of the handsome young man on the wall.

"He wouldn't marry me until his younger sister was grown. Both their parents were dead, and he felt the responsibility of providing for her." She laughed, a bitter sound. "He was worried about providing for a sister and a wife. Turnips and onions! I need no food at all. But he didn't understand. That was the price of both our happiness. Turnips and onions."

I nodded to show her I was listening. I could understand, at least in some way. The littlest things ruin lives. A faulty carriage wheel, a misshod horse . . . something such as this cost me my parents, and all my happiness.

Beryl continued. "We met in the woods one day. He was a timberman by trade. I pleaded with him to marry me and take me away from the miserable old widow. I promised I'd be a second mother to his little sister. But he would not bend."

She closed her eyes. "I grew angry. I told him I could have offered him endless life—and I could have. He said he had to get along with his work. We . . . struggled over the handle of his axe. I was just trying to make him stay, stay a little longer to listen, so that perhaps I could persuade him. He . . . he saw my strength and grew frightened of me."

Beryl sat very still.

"All his love for me drained out in that moment when he began to fear me. He turned and ran, leaving the axe in my hands."

Even knowing how this tale must end, I dreaded it. I closed my eyes.

"I hated him for fearing me. For abandoning me, when I'd done nothing but love him."

Please, make it end. I couldn't bear this story. Even behind my closed eyes, the portrait of the smiling youth lay before me.

"It was so sudden. *I was young, Lucinda!* Too young for my body, for my strength. All in an instant, I wanted to wound him like he'd wounded me."

I couldn't say I'd never felt that way toward Aunt.

"I threw the axe after him. It found its mark."

The bloodred flowers in the picture became the young man's blood, spilled on the ground around him.

Beryl's voice pleaded with me. "I didn't understand about dying. I didn't know what would happen to him."

If she came from a world where there was no death, she might well not understand. Pity for Beryl flowed over me. And yet, I couldn't allow her excuse to stand on its own. "But you knew you wanted to hurt him."

She nodded. "That is true."

"And the little girl?"

She turned and looked at me sharply. "What little girl?"

I pointed to the portrait on the wall. "The little girl who looks just like the young man you killed."

She hung her head.

"A sister?" I asked.

She nodded. "She found the body."

If I pitied Beryl, I pitied this poor child far more. An orphan, like me, but at least she'd had a brother to look after her, until this happened.

"What did you do for her?" I asked.

Beryl looked at me curiously. "What do you mean?"

I gestured impatiently. "Did you . . . apologize to her? Tell her what happened? Help her in some way?"

Beryl frowned. "If I had told her, or anyone, they would have tried to arrest me and hang me."

"And?"

She spread out her hands as if this should be obvious. "And it wouldn't have worked. No prison could hold me, no noose could kill me. So it was better for everyone that I went away, wasn't it?"

"Hmm," I said. "But what about the girl?"

Beryl sat a little taller. "I have kept watch on her, through the years, from a distance," she said. "She doesn't know me."

"You need to change that," I said, feeling reckless in the extreme. Who was I to chastise an immortal who has killed? "You need to apologize to her."

Beryl stared back at me, her head held high, her face haughty and cold.

"What good would it do?"

Suddenly I was the little girl.

"Much good, perhaps," I said. "Look at her face! You painted it yourself. Was there no one who ever explained to her the reason her brother was taken away?"

Beryl's arms were tightly folded across her chest again. She wouldn't look at me.

"It was decades ago. Almost a lifetime to the girl. Why dig it up again?"

I stared at Beryl until she was forced to look back at me. "Because she's suffered far too long already. Even if she's grown old now, she deserves to know."

Beryl sat motionless for a long moment. Then, to my great surprise, she crumpled, falling back weakly against the arm of the couch.

"Perhaps it would bring her some peace," she said thoughtfully, "regardless of what it does to me."

My fervor subsided. She meant it.

She reached for my hands. "Lucinda, if I can make some restitution, and if you can bring back my stone, it may be that I can find a way to be content here." She looked around the room. "I have my painting, and reading, and . . ." Her violet eyes pleaded with me. "I think I have . . . perhaps you and I will, in time, be . . . ?"

Friends.

I looked back at the paintings on the wall, of Mama and Papa, and me as a child, and felt a rush of hope. If I could track down Peter somehow, and find that stone, and relieve him of it, one way or another, this home was mine again!

I looked once more at the painting of the glorious youth, and the sorrowing girl. Her face haunted me.

"Who is she, Beryl?" I said. "The little girl?"

"Hortensia," Beryl said, watching me closely. "Hortensia Montescue. I believe you call her Aunt."

Chapter 12

How could I sleep after that?

But sleep I did. I tumbled into bed and passed immediately into a fitful slumber, dreaming urgent, fretful dreams, full of sorrow, but in the morning they mercifully faded from my mind. Dog slept on the foot of my bed, and that was a comfort, even if his hooves did bash my shins as he ran in his dreams.

When at last I rose, there was a fire to revive and water to heat. In all my preparations for venturing into the city, I soon forgot about my troubled sleep. I bathed in front of the fire in my room, where my nurse used to wash me. Never in all my years with Aunt and Uncle had I had a bath by a fire. And such elegant soap! Scented with lilacs. It smelled like Mama. I soaked and scrubbed my hair until it squeaked. It felt like years of grime and weariness sloughed off me. Dog helped by drinking from the tub.

I trimmed my hair and my nails and rubbed ointment into my chapped hands. Then I hunted down my mother's closets and found to my surprise that many of her clothes were still there, and none the worse for wear after a bit of sponging and ironing. I remembered almost every gown. It brought tears to my eyes to see them hanging limp in the closet, not worn by Mama. The one I chose, a blue merino winter dress with lace over the front, smelled of lilacs, too. It made my skin tingle to put it on.

I found boots and stockings and a coat and gloves, all somewhat faded and rumpled but still usable, and finer than anything I'd ever worn. I couldn't resist twisting my hair into an elegant coif and fastening on one of Mama's stylish little hats with hairpins.

I stood before Mama's dressing room mirror and spun around. In spite of everything, I laughed at the sheer joy of feeling clean and new. And fancy! Maybe, even, almost pretty. I took a closer look. In a mirror grainy and yellow with age I saw a face I'd never seen before, except as a shadow in the glass of Uncle's shop cabinets.

That shadow girl looked nothing like this one. This girl in the mirror looked like one for whom anything was possible.

I sat upon the cushioned chair and opened the small dresser drawer where Mama had kept some of her jewelry. Empty, of course. Whoever disposed of Mama and Papa's estate would doubtless have found the jewels in this drawer and sold them off long ago, to settle their debts, I supposed. Any fragments of value my parents left would have been picked over by vultures.

That was when the tears came. They rose from nowhere and waylaid me. The kind of tears I used to cry years ago, when their faces were still fresh in my mind and their loss was still something I believed might be a bad dream erased by sunrise.

My hand was still in the empty drawer. I slid it farther back, and the tip of my finger felt something hard and irregular in a corner. I yanked the drawer farther. Wedged in a crack where the wooden sides of the drawer joined was a cameo brooch. I brushed the dust away, revealing a serene figure, the delicately carved bust of a girl, immortally beautiful in her ivory stillness.

Just as Mama was immortally beautiful in my memories of her, in this very seat.

I pinned it to the lace at the throat of my gown, wiped my eyes, and went downstairs.

The house seemed empty. I searched through the kitchens for something to eat. Sunlight poured in through large windows, illuminating the small red petals of dozens of potted flowers that blossomed on the sills. The air was warm and moist, sweet with their perfume.

But there wasn't a bite of food to be found. Every cupboard was empty, save for tarnished pots. Nothing in the dairy, nothing in the cellars. I wondered how Beryl conjured up the soup she'd fed me.

She entered the kitchen as I banged cupboard doors. I felt myself stiffen, full of shyness after all she'd revealed to me last night. She, too, took in my appearance and smiled, a little nervously.

"You look lovely."

I thought it better, at this early hour, to be brusque rather than intimate. "Don't sound so surprised. Do you have any bread?"

She shook her head.

"Don't you eat?"

She gave a little *hmph,* half a laugh without the mirth. "I can eat," she said, "but I don't need to. This way there are no mice."

I dropped the lid to the empty flour barrel. "Well, I need to eat," I said. "Regularly."

She nodded. "I'll order some food."

"How?"

She gestured out the window and across a meadow. "A farmer and his wife live across the way. They help me keep up the property. I don't need the cooking or heating or washing that others do, nor do I keep animals, but the house and gardens need some tending."

I thought of the dozens of servants my parents had employed. Some tending indeed.

"Ben and Leda don't mind the pale color of my skin, and they like the color of my coins," Beryl said. "They'll find something to suit you."

"I'm not choosy," I said.

"In the meantime," Beryl said, reaching under the front placket of her dress and pulling out a pouch, "you may need to buy back the stone from whoever now holds it. There's plenty there for you to buy today's food in the city."

I took the leather pouch. Inside was more gold than I'd ever seen in one place, and she'd given it to me as casually as if it were a bag of hazelnuts.

"Where did you get such wealth?" I asked.

She smiled again. "Do you remember I said that when I came down the well, I'd been gathering pebbles from the riverbed?"

I nodded.

"Pebbles in our world are emeralds and rubies in yours," she said. "Each about the size of my missing gem. I had a sultan's fortune in my pocket."

I whistled. I knew enough after living with Uncle to know that kings fought wars over gems such as that. I jiggled the pouch of gold to hear it clink.

"How do you know I won't disappear with this gold and live off it forevermore?" I asked, half-jesting, half-curious.

"I don't know," she said.

And yet she trusted me, I felt sure of it. Aunt never trusted me an inch.

"Your flowers are pretty," I said.

She stroked a cluster of blossoms. "They remind me of home," she said.

I could well believe it. "What are they?"

"Can you guess?"

"I don't . . ." I stopped, remembering. It made me blush to say it. "Love-lies-bleeding?"

"That's right," she said. "Amaranth."

◆ ◆ ◆

Dog and I set out for the city and soon crossed the St. Justus Bridge. Beryl's money pouch jangled against my hip. I tried to hold it still so as not to attract the attention of pickpockets. Though perhaps, I thought, the attention of pickpockets is just what I should seek, since I was searching for one in particular.

As I walked, I considered Beryl's parting words to me. "Remember, Lucinda," she said. "Someone is searching for my stone. I don't know who. Please, be careful."

Wonderful. Not only did I face impossible odds, but I was competing with another, one who might—who knew?—hurt someone who stood in his way.

A blue sky hung over the first day of the Winter Festival. The air was colder, but the sun shone, warming my spirits. Perhaps I'd set out on a doomed errand, but I was clean as an apple and dressed like a lady, with the money to prove it.

I went to the first steaming cart I saw and bought a short loaf of bread with a crackling hot sausage tucked inside. The grinning vendor looked surprised at the coin

I'd handed him. I wondered if I'd made an improper meal choice for a young lady. But when my first bite of sausage exploded with hot juice, I didn't care.

My hunger satisfied, I took a hard look around and tried to form a plan. I'd never seen so many people in one place in all my life, and the crowd fairly overwhelmed me. How in this never-ending jostle of faces and noises could I find one thin young man? To be sure, there were skinny youths aplenty. That was part of the problem. Which of all these boots and trousers and spotty faces belonged to Peter—if that was even his name?

Hours passed. The sun began its descent. Only a few more hours of daylight.

I searched. I scanned faces. I walked until my feet were sore and my nose frozen. And still the sun descended, almost resting atop the tallest buildings on the horizon.

I drifted with the crowd to the center of town, where the city common had become an ocean of tents and carts and booths, some selling wares, others hot meals, and still others touting contests of skill and chance. Jugglers, clowns, and fools wove throughout the flotsam. The noise and commotion pressed upon me. Whenever my glance pointed west, the sun blinded me. The charm of the festival had faded hours before. I wanted to run away and seek sanctuary from the chaos. This wasn't a lark anymore.

Peter had to be in this crowd somewhere, but I began to doubt I'd ever find him.

At one end of the common a pavilion had been erected, with a platform and a podium. An orchestra seated on the platform played a tune that I could barely hear over the clapping. I'd so rarely heard any music at all since my parents died. I left Dog by a watering trough with instructions to wait—knowing him, he might understand—and pressed in for a closer look.

I wormed and elbowed my way through, one hand firmly clutching my purse, until I found myself at the edge of the crowd, almost tumbling into the patterns of a great dance. Men and women, young and old, ragged and neat, were lined up in pairs of rows, facing each other and holding hands with the person on either side. As the orchestra played, rows skipped to the right, then back, to the left, then back, came forward until the rows met, then stepped back again. People linked elbows and changed partners. Cheeks were red and smiling, breath blowing out in frosty puffs.

The dance charmed me—such order, such beauty, in the midst of the city's chaos! How was it possible for so many people to act in concert? I'd never known even three people to do it.

"What dance is this?" I asked an old woman.

"The gavotte," she said, shouting over the clapping. "They just finished the saraband."

The gavotte. I'd never seen one before. I clapped my hands and watched, letting the gaiety carry me with it. I wished I knew the steps. I envied the dancers.

Then a hand grabbed mine and pulled me into the dance.

It was so unexpected that I almost fell. Just my luck, to collapse and knock down a whole row of people! But the hand that grabbed mine wouldn't let me fall. I righted myself and jerked at the hand while it led me right then shoved me left. It belonged to a young man.

"I don't know the dance!" I protested, trying to get a look at his face.

He turned to look at me with laughing eyes. "That's obvious."

My tongue froze to the roof of my mouth.

Looking straight at me from under the brim of a mauve hat . . .

Was the prince.

"You!" I gasped.

"Me," he agreed, looking amused.

Underneath my mother's glove, the hand that held his began to sweat.

"I . . . I . . ." I was completely at a loss. He pulled me right, then guided me left, and I stumbled along, speechless and idiotic. He smelled of perfume and fur and mint, and looked even more carved from sunlight up close.

"Do I know you?" he asked, his eyes moving back and forth over my face.

"No," I blurted. "No, definitely not, no." I blinked, and

panicked. You don't just talk that way to royalty! "Your Highness! No, Your Highness, sir, we haven't. Met. Sir." I attempted a curtsy, which didn't fit into the gavotte at all.

His expression darkened and he looked away.

Was I that different in my mother's dress? Or just that easily forgotten?

I focused hard on the dance. If all these folk could do it, then so could I. And I was determined not to be any more foolish than I was already, in his eyes.

"You learn quickly," he said, smiling once more, which made my heart and my stomach change places.

"I like music," I said.

Who didn't like music, nonny-head? But his eyes were kind and didn't mock.

Our row of dancers hopped forward and bowed to those opposite us. The prince bowed to a red-haired young lady who blushed and beamed without once making an imbecile of herself, curse her.

The music neared its end. The prince examined me once more, and my insides turned to jelly.

"Are you sure we haven't met? Because you remind me so much of . . ."

"Of whom?" The words flew out before I could stop them.

"That's just it. I can't remember. Someone, maybe, from my childhood."

We hooked elbows and circled around each other, but

he made no move to change partners. The red-haired girl, now on my side, looked none too happy about it.

"Don't you think your childhood friends would have taken more dance lessons than I?"

He smiled. "Not necessarily. What have you studied?"

I stared at the ground. Not pianoforte, not dance, not painting silk screens, nor needlework nor deportment nor anything a young lady of quality should know.

"Jewelry," I said softly. His eyes brightened.

The song ended, and we bowed to each other, then clapped for the orchestra.

"I'm a bit of a collector myself," he shouted over the applause. "I've got some marvelous gems I could show you. A diamond they say is the largest ever to come out of India."

"Diamonds say 'forever,'" I said. The applause had only then dried up, so my words were a shout. I bit my tongue.

His eyes narrowed. "You don't say."

Had I ruined everything? I looked away. A crowd of young ladies surged up behind him, panting for their chance to address him.

He took my arm and pulled me close so he could speak in my ear. "What's your name?"

I stalled. I could forget to answer, just feeling him this close. I hadn't given any thought to divulging my name or not. Certainly not to the prince, whose family had been intimates of mine, once upon a time.

A pair of guards detached themselves from the crowd

and stepped forward to stand at the prince's side. Directly behind one of them, I caught a glimpse of a face disappearing behind a stout old lady.

Not now! Here I was in heaven, and yards away stood the devil I was chasing.

"Peter," I breathed.

"Peter?" the prince asked, surprised. "Miss Peter? Miss Peters?"

"No," I said, pulling away. "I mean, yes. Miss Peters. Miss . . . Angelica Peters. Good-bye!"

I darted off in the direction I'd seen Peter go, relieved to get away from the staring eyes that surrounded the prince. Then it hit me. I'd been rude to him on my first, my second, and undoubtedly my only encounters with him in life, and I'd run off with all the grace of a buffoon.

I turned back for one last look. It was too late. All I could see was the nodding crown of his hat over the cluster of people that surrounded him.

I turned back. There was no sign of Peter.

How could I lose everything, *everything* in one instant?

A trumpet fanfare rang out from the platform. The crowd grew quieter, and an announcer bellowed, "Hear ye, hear ye! The next song is a tribute to the Princess Beatrix of Hilarion, composed at his majesty Prince Gregor's special request! It will be played again tomorrow night at the royal ball celebrating their betrothal. Ladies and gentleman, I give you, 'The Pearldrop Concerto!'"

Applause rang out, and the lines of dancers collapsed into the crowd, all but where the Prince stood, his guards keeping a protective space around him.

"And here to grace the first public performance of the piece is the lady herself, Her Royal Highness Princess Beatrix!"

The applause went wild.

A guard dressed in green and yellow, the royal colors of Hilarion, ascended the platform, followed by a retinue of ladies in billowing gowns and fur stoles. They parted like flower petals to reveal an even more glorious lady, obviously the princess. She was petite, with white-powdered cheeks and a tower of flaxen hair elegantly arranged, with a peacock feather swooning over the top and brushing her forehead. Her furs were white, and they parted to reveal a sky-blue gown with skirts and flounces billowing widely from her tiny waist.

All around me were gasps and whispers.

"Ain't she beautiful?"

"Like an angel!"

"She's no bigger'n my ten-year-old daughter!"

"Aye, but she's full bloomed, ye can see that!"

The princess waved a gloved hand to the crowd and blew them kisses. Roses landed miraculously at her feet, though where anyone got roses at this time of year, I couldn't imagine. Her ladies gathered them up and presented them to her. She inhaled deeply from the bouquet and smiled prettily at the crowd.

Like an angel. Like a fairy princess. Like something sculpted from spun sugar to adorn a wedding cake.

I hated her.

"They'll make a handsome couple, those two," my tormentors continued. "I hear tell the prince is so much in love he can scarcely sleep nights."

Of course he was. How could he not be desperately in love with such an exquisite creature? Regal, beautiful, wealthy, destined for him. An irresistible combination.

Well? What did I expect?

Nothing! That was the worst of it. I was less than a nothing to someone like Prince Gregor, and I knew it. I'd only laid eyes on him twice, for the love of heaven.

But twice was enough.

At least I had danced with him—if my part could be called dancing.

I turned my back to the stage and willed myself not to look back at the prince again. Princess Beatrix had clearly been groomed since the cradle to be a queen, and that was the kind of bride he needed. And deserved. Good luck to them both.

The orchestra struck up the opening chords of the concerto. I scanned faces, searching for Peter, and had all but given up, when suddenly, there he was, at the edge of the crowd, staring dumbstruck at the stage. No doubt he was estimating the value of the princess's jewelry and forming a plan to steal it. I sidled my way through the crowd until I was directly behind him.

He wore a tricornered cap with the point pulled low over his right eye. When he turned his head slightly, I knew for certain it was him. The mark snaking down his cheek confirmed it.

I never thought, after that day that he ransacked my bedroom and my breakfast, that I'd ever feel this relieved to see him again. I'd found him! And now here he stood, every brazen inch of him, and all my old anger smoldered. How dare he steal from me, after I'd helped him hide?

Perhaps the jewel was still in his pocket. If not, he could surely take me to it. A little money, a little persuasion, and my quest would be complete, my childhood home mine, forever.

His attention was still fixed on the princess. I stood on tiptoe so I could speak directly into his ear.

"You shouldn't let your guard down, Peter," I whispered. "No telling who might sneak up on you."

He whipped around, his hand at his pocket, and scanned me up and down.

"And how do you know my name?"

"You took something of mine," I said, "and I want it back."

Chapter 13

Peter took off faster than an eel through bulrushes.

Perhaps startling him wasn't the shrewdest way to announce myself. But I hadn't come this far to lose now.

I lunged after him. He was quicker than me, but whereas he had to plow a path through the crowd, I merely followed his steps in the path he'd just cleared. In a footrace I'd never have kept up with him, but in all the bustle of the Winter Festival I managed to keep him in my sights, barely. Once, I came close enough to clutch at his arm, but he squirmed free.

"Come back!" I yelled. "Stop him!" But nobody listened.

Men hollered as we barreled past. Others joked loudly about a girl sprinting after a boy. Should be the other way around, they said. As if I'd ever chase Peter in *that* way!

Still, Peter ran away from the city center, elbowing his

way through festival goers. The sky had deepened from blue to purple, and the dying sun left an orange gleam at the edge of the world, just enough to throw long shadows across my path.

My chest cramped from the cold. As the crowds thinned, Peter began pulling away from me. Despair nearly choked me, but fury made me push each foot forward.

But I was losing. I couldn't stop my feet from slowing down. His legs kept pumping, though, and I felt a sob rise in my throat.

I could think of only one more thing to do.

"You stole something from me, Peter Thief," I yelled, "but I've come to buy it back!"

He stopped and turned, eyeing me suspiciously.

"Buy?"

I nodded. That *would* get his attention. Well done.

My legs throbbed, my chest burned. For half a penny I'd have laid down in the gutter. Not a pleasant place in the shabby part of town our chase had led us to, where kitchen waste and worse were dumped into the streets.

Slowly Peter approached, tacking back and forth as if undecided, keeping me firmly in his sights. He reminded me of Perdition, Aunt's cat, closing in on a mouse.

He frowned. "Who are you?"

I pulled off my hat, which was skewed from running, and worried the pins from my hair. "Don't you know me, then?"

He shook his head, but slowly this time, less sure of himself.

"Lucinda," I said. "From the goldsmith's shop? On Feldspar Street?"

His eyes widened.

"Two nights ago you slept in my bedroom," I said, irritated. "I should think that would leave some impression on you."

Now he knew me, it was plain. Just as quickly, he slid into his old lazy, mocking manner I'd seen in my garret. "Another night, another stop, another girl," he said. "After a while they start to blur together."

"What rot!"

Peter looked me over from side to side, circling behind me like a buyer inspecting a donkey. "Hallo there," he said, grinning, "so it is you, isn't it? I'd never know you in all that frippery." He rubbed his forehead with a dingy kerchief. "You could have told me who you were back there, and spared us both the exercise. How was I supposed to recognize you? You didn't have these fancy duds yesterday, I can say that." He fingered the woolen sleeve of my dress.

I yanked it away. "You're soiling my cuffs."

Peter ignored me. "Who's your friend?"

I felt a bony prod at my legs, and looked down to see that Dog had managed to follow me on my chase through the crowd.

"You're a miracle," I said, scratching between his horns. "This is Dog," I told Peter.

"Obviously," Peter said, raising one eyebrow. "Now, what's this about buying something back from me? I have plenty to sell, and I'm always happy to talk with people with cash."

I jingled the bag at my hip. "I've got cash."

Uh-oh.

A foolish slip. The gleam in his eyes confirmed it. I wrapped a hand around the mouth of the little money sack and squeezed it tight. A thief was a thief, and that was why I was in trouble in the first place. All my anger bubbled up once more.

"You stole something valuable from my pocket," I said. "Right out from under my nose, after I'd helped you and kept you as a guest in my room."

A group of drunken men spilled out the door of a public house close by, which had just lit its lamps. The evening air chilled my sweat and I shivered. Peter moved to my side and steered me by my elbow a little farther down the street, for all the world as though he were my beau.

"A word of critique," he said. "You have a tiresome way of rehashing old obligations and favors. A gentleman will grow weary of it. I feel as though we've had this conversation before."

I shook my arm free from his grasp.

"Tiresome? Because I don't think hospitality should be

rewarded with stealing someone's most valuable treasures?"

"See, now, there you go," he said. "What treasures? Where's the evidence? How often do poor servant girls like you have anything worth taking?"

"Servant girl?" He was more right than not. Still, I made a point of throwing back my shoulders and preening a bit in Mama's fine clothes. "It doesn't matter why I had it. The fact is, I had it, until you stole it."

"Baseless accusations. You have no proof that I took something from you."

I felt as though my veins would burst.

"Why, you . . ."

"Shh," he said, indicating the curious glances of people passing by.

"This is my proof," I hissed. "It was in my pocket until you came. You stole bread from my apron. You were the only person with access to me. I didn't lose it—the thief substituted a pebble for it."

Peter's lips twitched. "A clever touch."

"I caught you in the very act of stealing my aunt's things!"

He waved that away. "Mere rubbish," he said. "She should thank me for ridding her of old refuse. It was hardly worth my bother."

"But my treasure was worth the bother," I said. "You stole it."

"No, I didn't."

I wanted to stamp my feet. "Yes, you did!"

"Didn't."

"Did."

He folded his arms across his chest. "Didn't."

My hands tingled with desire to shake him until his teeth rattled. It's what came of growing up with Aunt. Always quick to try violence before reason. But he'd be too slippery to grab, that was sure.

Instead, I made as if to leave.

"Why you persist in this idiotic charade, I don't know," I told him, with all the condescension I could muster. "I know the truth, you know full well I do. But never mind. If you didn't steal it, then you won't be able to return it to collect the reward money."

I walked away, jingling my pouch. It didn't merely tinkle, like a bag with a few coppers. Its hefty *chunk, chunk* proclaimed its authority. Would Peter take the bait?

I hadn't gone five steps before I heard Peter's footfall behind me.

"Hold a bit," he said, cajoling. "Supposing—just supposing—I had an idea of where your gem might be found. Then what?"

He rested a would-be friendly hand on my shoulder.

I turned and jabbed my finger into his breastbone. "Who said anything about a gem?"

His Adam's apple bobbed.

"You knew it was a gem because you took it, you light-fingered bandit! You take everything good that isn't bolted down."

He rubbed the spot where I'd poked him. "And some things that are, to be truthful."

"Oh, why start being truthful now?"

"Because you've got a sackful of money," he said. "I'm a practical man. Not above telling the truth when it's the most profitable course."

"Tell it, then," I pleaded, "and we can be rid of each other forever."

"What, when we're getting on so well?" he said. He took me by the arm and started leading me back toward the heart of the festival. "The truth'll cost you supper, and I know just the place."

◆　◆　◆

Twilight continued to fold into night, and the sky grew blacker and deeper. We had only a patchwork of lamplight thrown from curtained windows to light our way back. But soon fires greeted us, built right in the center of the stone streets, and in rusty kettles beside buildings. Men carried torches, and every stage and stall was lit with lamps and hanging lanterns that swayed.

Night threw the festival into strange relief. Children had been scurried off to bed, and horses and carriages put to rest in stables. Now the streets were fair game for dancing, and the revelry took a turn as shadows crawled out from hiding to join the carousing. Laughter louder, music wilder, faces bolder. I was actually glad of Peter's arm in mine.

"See she caught you, lad," said a large man, appearing from the darkness like a ghost. His booming laugh made me jump.

"Aye." Peter grinned. "Sometimes it's better to be caught."

"Not by the constables, eh?" The man roared at his joke, smelling strongly of ale. I shied away from him and pressed forward.

"Here we are," Peter said, gesturing toward a glowing mountain of coals. Beside it a sweating one-legged man stood cranking the wheel of a curious apparatus that rotated several spits at once. Each spit held half a dozen plump, browning fowl, their juices dripping and sizzling on the embers, smelling deliciously of gravy and woodsmoke.

"Dinner for two, Poke," Peter said, with an affected wave of his hand. "Use the fancy china, will you?"

"Anything for your majesties," the man called Poke replied, with a mock bow. "But first, let's see your metal."

Peter elbowed me, and I opened my pouch, turning as far away from him as I could. I gave Poke a gold piece, and his eyes grew wide.

"The lady pays, does she?" He bent low and whispered in my ear. "I've known that Peter since he was a tot, and I warn you, he'll have that gold off of you in two shakes.

How's a nice young lady like you come to take company with the biggest rascal in Saint Sebastien?"

"Grim necessity," I said, and he roared with laughter.

It took most of his pocketful to give me change. Then he unhitched a spit from his strange machine and deftly slid off a bird onto a wooden board already shiny with grease. He cut the bird in half in one swift slice, skewered two steaming potatoes from a pan in the coals, and served us on trenchers of questionable cleanliness.

"Compliments to the chef," I said, breathing in the warm vapor. Poke grinned.

I could grow accustomed to regular hot meals, I decided. If all went well with Peter, I'd have them forever, with clean plate and cutlery, too. Mama's plate and cutlery. *My* plate and cutlery.

Peter steered me toward a watering trough, and we sat on its broad edge while Dog drank noisily. My day of searching and my chase after Peter had left me ravenous, and for a moment neither of us spoke, but took full advantage of Poke's skill. The hot potato burned my tongue then melted in my mouth, and the chicken . . . suffice it to say I did not eat it in a manner befitting the elegant lady I was dressed to be. Mama would not approve. Mama would never know.

People passed by in twos and threes, laughing loudly, their breath making frosty clouds before their faces. Groups of women began to appear, dressed in gaudy clothes. Their lips and cheeks, I was astonished to see, were painted with rouge, their eyes rimmed with black, and they wore large earrings that hung down to their nearly-bare shoulders. With a shock I realized what they must be, something I'd only encountered before in books.

"Evening, Maud," Peter called to one, a young blonde.

"Go on, you ruffian," she called back, laughing.

He'd called her by her first name! I watched her pass with a pair of comrades. Their shoulders, so white against the dark night, looked terribly cold.

I forced my attention back upon my food. At length, my energy restored, I remembered my purpose. Peter was still working on a drumstick when I asked, "Do you still have the jewel?"

I could see him calculating. He chewed and chewed, and licked his lips. "Not on me."

"Do you know where it is?"

"Approximately."

I snatched at his half-finished plate. "I'm weary of your games and lies. 'Supper for the truth,' you said, and I've paid my price. Now do you know where it is, or not?"

He shrugged. "Approximately, I said, and I meant it."

Dog sniffed at Peter's plate. It was tempting to give it to him. Instead, I willed myself to think coherently.

"Do you know who has it, then?"

"Most likely." He made a grab for his dish, but I held it at arm's length behind me.

"How can you most likely know who has it?"

"I know who had it when last I saw it."

"And when was that?"

"Last night. Late."

I'd rather interrogate someone who spoke a different language than try to wring the truth out of Peter. I took a deep breath, and spoke slowly and distinctly.

"And who had it last night, late, Peter?"

"My customer."

"Your customer. You sold it?"

"'Course."

He did a tidy turnaround, that one. If Uncle had done half as well, perhaps Aunt wouldn't have harangued him so much. Already sold it! Was there any hope now?

"How much did you sell it for?" I knew I'd get no honest answer.

He pursed his lips and scratched his head. "Can't say as I recollect exactly."

"Your razor-sharp brain's gone suddenly soft, has it? And I suppose you've already forgotten who your customer was?"

He reached a long arm over to snatch back his chicken. "I remember that well enough."

One last hope. "Then will you for the love of heaven tell me?"

"Not for that, but possibly for the contents of your bag." His feral smile made me clutch the purse tighter.

"You'll have this bag and all its contents once you've stolen my gem back from whoever you sold it to," I said.

He put up a flat palm. "That would be unsporting," he said. "When Peter sells, Peter doesn't take back. My clients would never trust me."

"Nobody trusts you!"

He had the nerve to look affronted. "Besides," he said, "I'd hang if they caught me stealing from this client."

The irony was too much for me. "That didn't stop you from stealing from me!"

He inclined his head in a small bow. "Pardon my saying so, but you're small fry compared to him."

My heart plummeted into my belly. If he wouldn't steal it back, however would I get it? Someone grand wouldn't be tempted by money. "Who'd you sell my jewel to? King Hubert?"

He smirked. He stalled. He took a long lick of his greasy fingers, a sight to turn anyone's stomach. All was truly lost now, and he was enjoying my suffering.

"Not quite," he said, "though give me time and I'll make a client of him, too. No," he said, gnawing on a bone, his eyes gleaming wickedly. "This time my client was only a shade less illustrious. I sold your spangle to Prince Gregor. He took a strange fancy to it. Said it'd be the perfect gift for his ladylove."

I felt as though a chunk of potato had lodged in my throat. I hadn't taken a bite.

"The princess?" I asked, trying to be casual.

Peter nodded. I saw a flash of annoyance on his face. "Why, what have you got against her?" I asked.

He frowned. "Nothing."

Something was going on under Peter's skin. I couldn't make it out, but it was a chink in his armor, which was all I needed. So I gambled.

I made an extravagant sigh. "It'd be a shame if Prince Gregor couldn't give Princess Beatrix a wedding gift, wouldn't it?"

He watched me under heavy-lidded eyes, saying nothing.

"And you won't steal it back for me, though by all rights you should, because you'd hang for it. I suppose I can't blame you for objecting to that."

He tilted his head, eyeing me from one side, much as Dog did.

A terrifying thought popped into my head. Tonight was a rash, reckless night, so I seized hold of it. "Of course, I could try to steal it back myself. . . ."

He snorted derisively. "You? Ha."

". . . if only there was someone who could teach me how it's done. A trainer. A tutor in thievery. For hire." I jingled my bag.

Lucinda, have you gone mad?

Odd strains of gypsy music floated out to us across the dark festival. I watched Peter's face through the shadows.

Once past the horror of his table manners, his face was a fascinating study in indecision.

"Supposing there was such a trainer," he said warily, "how much would he be paid?"

I met his gaze. "Everything I've got here, as soon as I've got the gem in my hands."

He shook his head. "No good. I can't be responsible for the outcome. Too risky."

"A third up front, then," I said, "and the rest upon the success of the mission."

"Half."

Why, why was I bargaining with a thief? Would he really be able to help me? Did I have a chance of success?

Now wasn't the time for caution. I couldn't afford it.

"Half."

Peter shifted in his seat. "And if anything goes wrong, or you get caught, you've got nothing to do with me, got that? I don't know you and I never taught you anything."

I tore a bite of chicken flesh from its bones. "Never anything."

Peter ate the last of his potato then put forth his hand. "Then I offer you my services."

I slapped my hand in his, chicken bone and all. "Deal."

Chapter 14

I counted out the coins on the stone edge of the watering trough. Peter insisted on watching; I insisted he stand far enough away that he couldn't touch.

"That's no way to show trust in your new advisor," he sniffed.

"Balderdash."

Once he'd pocketed the coins, and I'd tied my much-lighter wallet securely back upon my belt, suddenly Peter was all business.

"Right then," he said. "First, you begin by knowing your target. I can help there. The prince believes the gem is magic. Romantic. Like a love charm." He laughed. "That idiot will believe anything I tell him."

I bristled. "He is not an idiot!"

Peter made a low whistle and shook his head. "So you're another one, are you?"

"Another one what?" I cursed myself for talking without thinking.

"Another of the empty-headed Saint Sebastien females who run around besotted by Prince Gregor's dimples and curls."

Thank heaven the darkness concealed my blushing.

I'd never thought of that. It made me feel sick. Of course I wasn't the first to look at him.

"Nothing of the kind," I snapped.

Peter grinned. "And how would you know if he's an idiot or not?"

Think fast! "I've heard tell of him."

Peter shrugged. "Anyway, he'll have it on his person, that's certain. He met the princess for the first time today. He's been all worked up about it." That, I knew. "So he'll have his love charm with him, sure as anything. And if I know him, it will be in his inside breast pocket." Peter gestured into his jacket with his hand.

That caught my attention. "How d'you know where he'd keep it? How would you know him so well?"

That same tight-lipped look I'd seen a moment before crossed his face and vanished as quickly, to be replaced by his usual sarcasm. "You mean, why would a gent like me keep such low company? I told you, he's my client."

"Yes, but you don't just have the prince as your client any old day of the week," I said.

"That's true," he said. "Only on days when I have something he'd want to buy."

"Does the king know that the prince buys stolen gems?"

"Not 'stolen,'" Peter said, elaborately pressing his fingertip and thumb together in an affected flourish under his nose. "Exclusive and sought after."

"Indeed."

"Time's wasting," he said, glancing around. "Quit interrupting the training."

"I'm not . . ."

"As I was saying, the prince thinks it's a love token, so he'll have it with him. He won't have given it to her yet, I'll wager. He'll be waiting for a more private opportunity."

I gasped.

"What?" Peter asked.

"Nothing," I said. *I've got some marvelous gems I could show you. A diamond they say is the largest ever to come out of India.*

"Peter," I said. "When you sold the stone to him, where did you say it was from?"

He scratched his head. "China? No. India. That's right."

I nodded.

"Adds to the perceived value. Why do you ask?"

"Just wondering."

"Yes, well, I wish you'd quit changing the subject. As I was about to say, the princess will likely be back at the palace by now. The festival by night is no place for respectable young ladies," he said, giving me a meaningful look. I pulled my coat tighter around me.

Peter continued. "By tradition, the prince will have

hosted the festival and the dancing all day long, which works to your advantage. He'll be exhausted. He'll have just stuffed himself at the banquet. Then there'll be more music and dancing afterward, though not the kind you saw earlier today. Now, pay attention."

I was already paying attention.

Peter chose a stone from the ground, wiped it, and dropped it into his pocket. "An inside pocket is difficult," he said. "And the prince is heavily guarded. If it were me picking it off him, I'd strike up a conversation with him, in the middle of a lot of commotion, lots of people all around, and at the right moment I'd direct his attention elsewhere, so he turns, see?" Peter demonstrated a dramatic turn to one side, as if he'd heard a cry of "Fire!"

"Now, watch here. Right at that moment, while he's turning, I'd slide in with one quick movement, grab the stone, and have it out before he's realized there's nothing to see." Peter demonstrated by robbing himself of a pebble.

"Impossible!" I said.

He shook his head. "You'll never make your living as a thief. That's the most elementary maneuver. I do it twice in a week at least."

I didn't doubt him.

"But you're not me," he continued, "and in this one case, therein lies your advantage. I'm not a girl. You are."

He looked at me as if he'd made a revelation. I was utterly baffled.

"Don't be a simpleton! What I mean is, you're a *girl*. You can flirt with him, cozy up to him, dance with him. He won't even notice a little tickle in his chest pocket." He grinned rakishly. "He'll probably like it."

I jumped up from the watering trough. "Just what kind of a girl do you think I am?"

He looked at me thoughtfully. "Truth be told, I couldn't say. One day you're sharing your bedroom with street thieves, next day you're nearly a duchess."

Sharing my . . . !

"At any rate, I don't see why it wouldn't work. You're not ugly."

I blinked. *Not* ugly? I could feel my face grow hot. I had no special delusions of beauty, but still.

He continued. "The prince won't be choosy. At festival, he'll dance with anyone."

Oh, better yet.

Once more, he looked me up and down. "I'll go so far as to say that the prince will find you quite amusing." He wagged a finger in my face. "We're not talking about marrying you off. We're talking about getting near to the prince for one minute, maybe two. Surely you can produce enough charms to manage that."

"Spoken from the lips of an expert on charm," I said.

"Why, thank you." He swept off his hat with a flourish. Then he patted the pebble in his coat pocket. "Let's practice. I'll be the prince. Approach me and try to get my attention."

I'd never felt so self-conscious in all my life. Peter watched me expectantly. Think of the house, I told myself. This was only a training exercise, one for which I'd paid a fortune. Might as well make the most of it.

"Hello, Your Highness," I attempted.

"No, no, no," he said. "Simper! Bat your eyelashes. Look at him this way," he looked at me out of the corner of his eyes, making a repulsive smile intended to look coy, then looked away. "Curtsy. Bow your head modestly." He contorted his neck grotesquely.

"You're about as modest as a tom turkey," I observed.

"I'm not female!" he said. "It'll come naturally to you."

There was no point favoring that remark with a reply. "Can't I just trip him and hope it flies out of his pocket?"

Peter rolled his eyes. "Amateurs," he muttered. "Now try again."

It's only Peter, I told myself. Just practice.

But when the real performance came, it wouldn't be Peter. It would be *him*.

My stomach flopped. Yes, I'd twice made a fool of myself around him, but not that kind of fool. Not a deceiver, and a thief.

He'll lose all respect for me.

He has no respect for me.

All these thoughts chased each other while Peter watched me, arms folded.

"Well?"

I took a deep breath. I closed my eyes and willed my mind not to think. I thought of the painted ladies passing by.

Now.

"Hello, Peter," I purred, half opening my eyes. "Don't you look *fine* tonight?" I fluttered my eyelids and turned my shoulders to show my profile to its best advantage—if, hypothetically speaking, my profile had any advantage, which I doubted.

Peter's mouth fell open.

I sidled closer to him.

"How long *has* it been since I saw you last?" I drawled, *soprano voce*. "I declare I almost fainted when I laid eyes on you just now. *Such* a sight for sore eyes." I rested one hand briefly on his shoulder. "Cold tonight, isn't it?"

Peter's eyes bulged. He swallowed hard and stepped back.

"Yes. Well. Very good." He straightened his collar and shook himself slightly. "Yes. Now let's just practice the filch." He indicated his jacket. "Try to get the stone without drawing attention to yourself."

Peter was about my height, which helped. He pretended to look away. With my left hand low, I tugged his lapel out just slightly. With my right, I slipped a hand into the pocket, grabbed the stone, and pulled it out.

"Good enough," Peter said. "Let's go."

"Wait," I said. "Let's try it again. I'm sure that wasn't

subtle enough. You could tell I was doing it, couldn't you?"

"Of course I could," Peter snapped. "I'm a professional, not an idiot prince who's had his vanity stroked. But you did fine. The prince won't notice. Let's go."

He grabbed my hand and started pulling me. Dog protested loudly.

"Your friend here will be no help at all," Peter said.

"You'll have to keep him with you," I said. Peter grimaced.

We handed Poke our trenchers as we passed by. His fowl spits were nearly bare. "A good night, eh, Poke?" Peter said.

He hustled me through the crowd, which had grown more dense and boisterous. Suddenly everyone seemed to be a large, loud man with a foaming mug in his hand, a bawdy song on his lips, and a feathered female on his arm.

My heart thumped and my insides felt like jelly. Lucinda Chapdelaine, what has come over you?

"Are you sure this is going to work?" I asked. "I've paid a lot for this training. I don't think I got enough practice."

"Too much practice makes you rigid," he said. "I work by instinct. Quick mind, quick eye, quick fingers. It's a way of thinking."

"I'm not used to that way of thinking," I grumbled.

Peter stopped and faced me severely. "If you want this

stone bad enough, you'll muster the right thinking whether you're used to it or not."

I nodded. He was right.

"Cheer up," he said, pressing forward once more. "If you're successful, I might let you work with me." He pointed through the throng. "Look. There he is."

Chapter 15

Unmistakably, there he was.

We were near the pavilion where the orchestra had played earlier that day. A group of gypsy musicians now occupied the stage, their music as wild and haunting as the other music had been ordered and smooth. There was still dancing going on, but not the gavotte. Women whirled, colored scarves trailing behind them like flaming serpents. Others clapped tambourines. Men stomped and clapped and shouted over the music.

The prince stood by a table loaded with food and drink, talking with a group of guards. At the sight of them my confidence, if I had any, drained away. Gregor set his plate down on the table and dropped it, splattering a guard with sauce. The others shouted with laughter.

Peter crouched behind me, his breath tickling my ear.

"He makes quite a figure, doesn't he?" he asked

maliciously. "I can't go any closer than this. We can't have him see me. I'll be over there"—he indicated an abandoned stall some distance behind where we stood—"trying to keep your goat away from you. That's a bonus, by the way, for which I could charge extra. Don't say I've never done anything for you."

My rising panic reached a crest. I spun around and clutched his sleeve.

"Peter, I can't do this," I said.

He looked me straight in the eye. I found it hard to match his gaze.

"It's no skin off my nose whether you do or don't," he said. He patted his jingling pocket, swollen with Beryl's gold, then tapped my forehead sharply with his pointer finger. "But I say that you can. And you will." He smiled at me.

"You'll be watching, won't you?" I asked.

"Promise."

Only slightly relieved, I turned back for a glance at the prince, who was laughing with a guard.

His face sent a stab of longing through me.

I turned back to look at Peter, but he was already gone. I scanned around for him, or even for Dog, but saw no trace of either of them.

What's a thief's promise worth, anyway?

If I succeeded, Peter would get the rest of my gold. Or perhaps he'd simply slip away, content with half. It was enough to make him a wealthy man, not to mention whatever price he'd gotten from Prince Gregor. Why did he dress so raggedly, and live on the streets? By what he'd collected in only a few days, he ought to live in comfort in an elegant townhouse.

One of Gregor's guards gestured toward a carriage. He might leave soon. By the looks of things, I didn't have long to try my new dramatic skills upon him.

Now or never. And if never, what would become of me?

I took a first fearful step.

I felt naked without Peter. Each step forward was an effort. I cut a swath of silence through the chaos, as conversations stopped and white eyes stared from bearded faces at the unescorted young gentlewoman (if only they knew!) on the city streets after dark at the festival. Their curiosity mingled with contempt. They formed an impenetrable wall around me.

Suddenly reaching the prince felt like my best option. He was the one person I knew in this wild assembly—if our acquaintance could be called "knowing." I fixed my eyes on his face and hurried forward.

And then, I was only a few feet away, and he turned and saw me, which was more frightening then facing the flock of wolves I'd just passed through. And now there was no turning back.

At the sight of me, he smiled, and I turned to jelly all over again. Pick *his* pocket? Was I mad?

"Miss Peters," he said, bowing.

He remembered my name! My un-name, that is.

His guards didn't bow, but their eyes took me in appraisingly.

"Can I assist you, Miss Peters?" Prince Gregor said, all politeness.

How many guards were there? A hundred? Half a dozen, to be sure, but all of them staring at me.

And Gregor, waiting for an answer. I had none to give him.

Got to get closer to him, away from these guards.

Music. Gypsy music.

"Dance!" I blurted.

Oh, help.

I thrust my chin out defiantly. "I came to dance."

A ripple of laughter passed through his guards. They winked at each other, and the nearest one elbowed Prince Gregor.

"I'll dance with her for you, Your Highness," he said. "Save you for the princess, eh?"

The night air was sharp, cold as the grave, but my cheeks burned.

I was trapped.

Gregor's expression was puzzled, but he offered me his hand. "That's all right, Rolf," he told the guard. "This lady is an acquaintance of mine. I claim the honor."

There was more laughing and waggling of eyebrows

among the guards, but Gregor led me away from them. Whispers followed us. Gregor's guards weren't the only ones amused by my audacity.

"Don't mind them," Gregor said. "It's just that no one's ever done that before."

I looked sidelong at him, searching for a bulge near his breast pocket. "Done what?"

He grinned. "Asked me to dance."

"Nonsense," I said. "Every girl in the kingdom is desperate to dance with you."

He stood opposite me, offering me his arms. "Shall we?" I put my hands in his. "The other girls, Miss Peters, I regret to say, have been taught they must wait to be asked."

Oh. All the blood drained from my face. I tried to follow Gregor's steps, despairing. All the while, his pockets were a full arm's length away.

"I didn't have time to wait," I said.

"How lucky for me," was his enigmatic reply. The corners of his mouth twitched. I studied his face, trying to determine whether he was mocking me. Well, of course he was mocking me, but with good humor or not, I couldn't tell. I didn't dare look too often at his face, lest I lose my head completely.

The gypsy music forced upon us a lively dancing pace that Gregor negotiated easily, but it left my petticoats in a tangle and put me at risk of toppling. I watched his feet, then looked down at my own, but they were lost in a sea of skirts. Whenever I glanced at Gregor, there was that suppressed laughter again. Curse his pampered hide, not everyone had spent a lifetime in lessons! How's a girl to pick a dancing prince's pocket when she can't even match his steps?

"You're no help," I said, too vexed to care whether or not he knew it. "Teach me!"

"First a dance, and now a lesson," he said. "You're a demanding creature, Miss Peters. Will there be anything else, while I'm at it? An invitation to dinner?"

"It's too late for dinner," I snapped. "All I need is one dance, with you."

Too late, I realized how brazen this sounded. I scrambled to save myself. "After this, I won't trouble you anymore."

Gregor raised my arm high and twirled me around. "That," he said, "would be unfortunate." Then he altered the dance. His arm went behind my waist, and my other hand, now free, had nowhere to rest but on his shoulder. I leaned my head back and watched the constellations revolve overhead till they blurred together. My whole body tingled with heat and shock at this frightening, dreamlike sensation of dancing. Close. To a painfully beautiful young man. Who was gazing down at me.

Then he stopped. A thought seemed to strike him. "Has someone put you up to this, Miss Peters? Is this a wager, or a joke?"

My conscience stung me. I remembered my bargain with Peter. Not quite a wager, but nearly.

"No," I said. "No wager. No joke."

Gregor rejoined the music, taking a grave hop-step to one side and then back to me. "Then what reason could you have," he mused, "for insisting upon a dance?"

Did he want me to say it was because he was handsome? I'd not give him that satisfaction. "Perhaps I'm a foreign spy, sent to observe the prince," I said.

Gregor's eyes sparkled. "Or," he said, "perhaps you're a common thief, come to pick my pockets."

I laughed, rather too shrilly, avoiding his eyes. My skin went slick with guilty sweat. "You've found me out."

Gregor flashed his magic smile, then pinned me with his sober gaze once more. "Why *did* you ask me to dance tonight?"

I had run out of lies. "Because," I said, my heart pounding, "tomorrow night would be too late."

I didn't dare look at him. Then, I couldn't help it. He was so close, the tip of his nose brushed mine. His breath was warm on my cheek. His eyes . . .

He caught himself suddenly, stiffened, pulled away. "Pardon me. I . . . I was trying to hear you better. The noise . . . But I'm neglecting your dancing lesson! Er, the name of this step is the *pas cabriolé*, and it's done by . . ."

He taught me until I'd done a passable *pas cabriolé*, a capering sort of step.

"Excellent!" he cried after a dismal attempt or two. I smiled back. He squeezed my hand. "Tomorrow's not too late for a dancing lesson. Come to the ball. We can continue our lessons there."

He wanted to see me again.

At the *palace ball*.

It was a lovely dream, but . . .

"Prince Gregor," I said, standing stock-still, "I can't. Tomorrow night is for the princess."

He seemed to lose an inch in height, but his grip on my waist tightened. "All the same," he said. "Come. Please."

I stalled for a clever reply. "I don't know if I'm interested in such dull company as the palace ball."

I felt, more than heard, the laughter in his chest. Suddenly I remembered my errand. This close, could I get my hand inside his pocket without him noticing? Maybe. But the music lulled me. Why risk it and wreck this moment? The stone wasn't going anywhere.

The song ended, and another began, slow and melancholy. I waited, breathless, for him to end our dancing, but before I'd heard two bars of the new tune, both of Gregor's arms were around me. I could feel his pulse in his jaw as he pressed his face next to mine.

"Thank you for demanding a dance, Miss Angelica Peters," he said in my ear. "I don't know when I've enjoyed myself more."

My body pounded inside its skin, like a windup toy in

a box. The bristles on his chin scraped against my cheek. I breathed in once more the scent of his cologne, and mint, and the fur trim on his coat. My eyes blurred. Swinging lanterns became dancing stars. The cold air melted into delicious heat.

We danced.

Somewhere in that song, I crossed a line in the sand. There would be no turning back. The thought of this night ending, the musicians packing up and going home to bed, taking with them my excuse to dance with Gregor, was more awful than I could bear. What did cold stones matter on a night like this?

Dear one, I cannot do to you the deed I intended to. For the gift of this moment, I will let you keep my only chance to be the somebody you suppose I am.

I will not steal the stone.

Drunk with longing, I wanted to give him something, a token of truth to remember me by.

"Call me . . . Lucinda, please," I said, suddenly shy. "It's the name my mother used for me." The only name she ever used for me.

"Lucinda," he said, experimentally. "Lucinda. Yes. It suits you."

Why did I feel more a liar than before? "I prefer it over Angelica," I said.

"So do I."

I shivered again, and Gregor stopped dancing, looking

at me with concern. He shrugged out of his coat and draped it over my shoulders.

"Wait here," he said. "I'll get you some punch."

I slid my arms inside the coat, feeling his warmth all over it. I watched his shirted back as he pressed toward one of the bonfires, where a brazier of hot wine simmered in the coals. The fire glowed around the edges of his shape, like a halo.

I buried my face in his ermine fur collar and tried to breathe in some of the happiness hanging like stardust in the air.

My fingers pulled the lapels tightly around me, and as they did, I felt a heavy lump in the inner pocket.

Beryl's stone.

*   *   *

I can't do this to him!

He'd handed me the chance. He'd never know. In spite of the onlookers, no one would see my hand slip out from under his jacket with a gem clenched in my fist.

I'd sworn to myself that I would not do it, but fate had intervened. Perhaps the stone itself, imbued with Beryl's power, intended to return to its owner. Perhaps when I resumed my rightful place in society I could restore to Gregor the loss I was now imposing upon him. Perhaps we could remain friends. Perhaps he'd need a friend who made him laugh.

Perhaps my life would be unendurable if I could never see Gregor again.

And I surely never would, with neither a home nor a penny to my name.

He was coming back, friendly concern for me written across his face. Under the cover of his coat, my fingers dug inside the pocket and pulled up the stone. I clenched it in my fist just as Gregor reached my side.

"Drink this," he said, handing me a steaming cup. I took it with my remaining hand and sipped too quickly, burning my lips.

"Careful," he said.

He raised his glass. "To Miss Peters—to Lucinda— may she live long and healthy, and may she dance with me again soon."

He watched my face nervously. My guilt swelled with each heartbeat, but somehow, I smiled back at him. He grinned back, relieved, and drank from his cup. Then he bent forward and swiftly kissed my cheek. The soft, damp touch lingered long after his lips were gone.

Beryl's stone burned in my hand. *Thief!* He kisses you, and you're robbing him?

Murmurs and laughs around us showed that others had seen him kiss me. He put his arm around me as if defying the crowd. He might defy them, but I wanted away from all those staring eyes.

"I'd better go," I said. "Thank you for the dancing

lesson. And for your coat." I slid my arms out, clutching my fist tightly so he couldn't see what it held.

"Wait! Don't go yet," he said, reluctant to take back his coat.

I had to flee, and yet, I couldn't leave without him knowing. I pushed the coat toward him, stood on tiptoe, heedless now of the whistles and jeers around me.

I heard the swift intake of his breath as my lips brushed his cheek.

"Good-bye," I whispered in his ear.

He clutched my arm. "Wait! Where do you live? How can I find you, send you a message?"

Out of the corner of my eye I saw Rolf approaching, worry written upon his face. Did Gregor's guards feel they should protect the prince from foolish love affairs, too?

"Thank you for tonight," I said. "I'll always remember it. But you don't need to find me. You know that."

"Your Highness," Rolf said, now standing beside Gregor, "it's time for us to go."

At the sight of his guard, Gregor deflated. He sighed.

"Rolf, do you remember meeting Miss Peters before?" Gregor asked. "Because I could swear I have, before today. And you're always there wherever I go, like a dratted nuisance, so if I'd seen her, you would have too."

Rolf took a long sideways look at me, and shook his head. "Can't say I have ever seen her, Highness."

I curtsyed to Gregor. "Thank you for the dance," I said. "I am most honored."

"The honor is all mine," Gregor said bitterly. "Come to the ball?" Rolf's eyes darted toward the prince's face.

It was time to go. No sense prolonging the moment, and no wish to, with Rolf's eyes on me. I squeezed Beryl's gem until my fingers ached. Now was the time to flee.

"Good evening, sirs," I said, curtsying once more. I turned to go, taking the first step toward success and freedom. Why, then, was it so hard to leave?

Yet with each step my confidence swelled, my spirits rose. I'd done it! I'd danced with him, I'd kissed him, and he me. He loved me, if only for a moment, and on top of all that, I'd gotten Beryl's gem back! There must have been an enchantment in the air tonight. Some star had smiled kindly upon me.

I quickened my steps. The flock of wolves held no terror for me now. Not while Gregor cared for me. Impossible, unbelievable miracle, beyond explanation, but true! He cared. For *me*. I could have flown home.

I searched for Peter's face. Still no sight of him. Gladly, gladly would I give him Beryl's gold now. And we would celebrate!

There he was, watching for me. I shook a triumphant fist in the air, and he grinned. I quickened my steps and ran toward him. Good old Peter, that scalawag, no liar was ever a truer friend. And all the strangers in the crowd— marvelous people! I loved them, too. Love was everywhere tonight. It flowed through me with plenty to spare for everyone. Gregor had kissed me! I could still feel the mark. I could feel how his whiskers had tickled my lips when I kissed him back.

A whistle pierced the darkness.

"Stop!" a deep voice roared. "Stop in the name of the king!"

I paused, looking around, wondering what had happened. A fight, perhaps?

"Thief!" a woman's voice cried. "Thief!"

A cold shock went over me. Please, heaven, let it be a woman whose earring was stolen.

Somehow, I didn't think so.

The voices and footsteps came nearer, and nearer. No sign of Peter now. I looked for a way to run, but now the crowd pressed thick around me, everyone looking to see what was wrong. I felt trapped in a labyrinth. If only these cobbled stones would open a crack and hide me! I tried to push forward, but a rough hand grabbed my wrist and spun me around.

A huge, thick-jawed constable stared down at me. Behind him a woman's shrill voice reached the skies.

"I saw her!" she yelled. "Bold as you please, dancing with the prince, then picking his coat pockets while he got her a drink!"

The hand that held the gem went numb. No place to hide it now.

"Let's see your hand there, girl," the constable ordered.

Trembling, I let my hand be taken and pried open.

"That ain't yours, I'll wager," he said, seizing the stone. "Is this what you saw her take, Madam?"

He turned and showed the stone to my accuser, who stepped forward into the beam of a lantern held by a curious onlooker.

"That's it, all right," said Aunt.

Chapter 16

The sight of her face was worse than any nightmare. Hot tears stung my eyes.

"Crying won't help you none," barked the constable. "That's a hanging offense, that is. Robbing royalty." He shook his head.

I looked to the woman I called Aunt, in whose home I'd served for ten years. Did she know me? Of course she did. Recognition and revenge blazed in her eyes. What was she doing here? Drinking Uncle's death away? She quivered with excitement.

Behind her, a commotion moved its way closer. Lanterns swung by eager onlookers converged upon me like moths to a flame. With a sickening heart I saw the prince and his guards approach. Gregor talked and smiled and pointed at me. With despair I realized he thought he was about to clear up a jolly mistake involving his new friend, Miss Peters. I hid my face behind my empty hands.

"Name?" the constable demanded.

Who was I?

Not this girl who'd been arrested for theft.

Angelica Peters, I thought to say. But Aunt spared me the trouble.

"Lucinda Chapdelaine," she announced to half the city.

Voices and laughter stilled. Even the music had stopped. All was silent, save for a rustle of whispers like wind through grass. The wolves and vixens stood in an accusing circle around me that stretched to the edge of the city common. If the sky had fallen on me, I could not have felt more suffocated.

The constable turned, surprised. "You know her?"

I felt a nudge at my ankles. It was Dog. My only friend. Hot tears spilled from my eyes.

"What's all this?" came a new voice. I looked. There stood Gregor, and beside him, to my great shock, was his father, King Hubert, whose image I knew from every coin that ever passed through our shop. It was he who spoke. "What did you say her name was?"

"Lucinda Chapdelaine," Aunt said, swelling like a bullfrog.

"Swiped this off the prince," the constable said, holding up Beryl's gem for all to see. A ripple of admiration ran around the ring of watchers.

Gregor's stricken face leaped out at me.

The king strode forward. The crowd parted before him.

He lifted my chin and looked into my face. "Chapdelaine," he said. "Not . . . August and Olivia Chapdelaine's child?"

"The very same," Aunt said, nodding.

My dream flooded back upon me, the memory of the banquet my parents hosted, where the king had promised me two dances with the prince. The sticky-faced prince who'd drunk too much punch.

His promise had been kept.

"Your Majesty," I said. "Please, let me explain."

King Hubert paid me no attention but turned and looked at Aunt. His face was puzzled. Aunt's shabby gray dress and shawl did not, apparently, fit with Mama's fancy clothes.

"How do you know this young lady?" he asked her.

She curtsyed deeply. "If it please Your Highness, she was my dear departed husband's niece, by marriage. I raised her up ever since her parents died bankrupt and left her penniless."

Beat me down, more like. It was only Uncle who gave me any hope worth living for.

"And you say that you saw her stealing something from my son?"

She nodded. "She's a thief by nature. I kicked her out of my house two days ago for stealing right out from under my nose at my goldsmith's shop. She didn't have a penny, Your Highness. Those clothes she's got on are stolen, sure as anything."

I watched Gregor. At the words "goldsmith's shop," he blinked. I saw his lips form the word "Lucinda." At last. He remembered the amusing girl from the shop. His eyes were full of bewilderment and betrayal.

"You kicked her out without a penny?" King Hubert asked.

Aunt cleared her throat. "She'd stolen from me, sire. Family heirlooms, and all the gold in the till."

"I did not!" I cried.

The constable seized the purse of gold from my waist and ripped it off.

"Got a sackful of it here," he said, fingering the contents of the bag.

Aunt gasped. "Why, that's my purse and all! Robbing the widow what cared for her when she was a poor orphan. Have you ever heard the like?"

The king looked at me. "What do you have to say for yourself?"

His face was unreadable, but at least, unlike Aunt's and the constable's, it wasn't full of loathing for me.

I looked at Gregor as I spoke.

"I never stole a thing from this woman in my life," I said with all the force I could summon. "I am wrongfully accused. A thief broke into her home and took some heirlooms, and she accused me. Nobody robbed the till. There was nothing in it to take."

The king gestured to the constable, who handed him Beryl's gem.

"Gregor," he called. The prince stepped forward. "Is this yours?"

Oh, please. You could save me, Prince. I begged him silently to look at me, but he would not.

"Yes, my lord," Gregor said after a pause.

So be it, then.

The king waved the gem under my nose. "Now, young lady, in the presence of all these witnesses, tell the truth. It will go better for you. Did you steal this from my son?"

I tried to moisten my tongue. I closed my eyes to block the hateful sight of all those accusing eyes. All evidence was against me, and there were no friends to rescue me. No Peter. My only friend was a goat.

I opened my eyes. "I did steal it, Your Highness," I said. "But if you'll permit me, I can explain."

The king shook his head sadly. "I can't tell you how this pains me, Miss Chapdelaine," he said. "Your parents were my good friends. To see their child come to this end is a deep source of grief."

"Her parents were dishonest, too," Aunt piped up. "Died in default on spurious loans. All that high living on credit and fraud!"

The king pressed his lips together. "That will do," he said. He waved a hand to the constable. "Lock her away, officer," he said. "Lord Coxley will tend to her case. She has pled guilty to theft against the crown. From the prince's very person, no less." He turned to Gregor. "Let this be a lesson to us both, son, that people are often not what they seem."

The constable seized my wrist once more and dragged me away. Dog butted him hard in the leg, and he kicked at him savagely. This brought loud laughter from the jury of spectators.

"Gregor, please!" I cried over the noise. "Let me explain!"

His eyes met mine, but his jaw was set. There was no room for me in his eyes.

"Listen to her taking liberties," Aunt cried. "Calling the Crown Prince by name!"

My last view of his face, seared across my mind, was cold and rigid and condemning. What warmth there had been was frozen, poisoned, gone.

How quickly love can turn to hate.

How easily the axe is thrown.

Chapter 17

If there ever was a time in my life when I wished I knew how to pray, or to whom I should pray, it was the ride in the constable's wagon from the common to the Hall of Justice. I couldn't fold my hands in supplication; they were tied behind my back, and none too gently.

My wrists chafed. The constable had stripped off my gloves, announcing that they'd do nicely for his missus. Then he took the reins, leaving me on the bench of the wagon and tossing back occasional insults as if they were comments on the weather.

No matter. My torment at the hands of this rude constable would be brief. And then they'd hang me.

Much as I'd resented the prying eyes and blinding lanterns of the crowd at the festival, when the wagon pulled away and left the throng behind, I yearned for those lights and faces. Now I was utterly without help.

This was why Peter refused to rob the prince. All that customer nonsense was pure rubbish. This is what Peter knew could happen to me, and he let me go forward with it. He watched my downfall, and as soon as the trouble fell, he disappeared.

And I had begun to imagine we were—almost—friends. What did I know of friendship?

Why, why did I change my mind and steal the stone after vowing not to? Did I really think by doing so I could have a chance at the prince? Not when there's a real princess about, made of crystal sugar, with a kingdom for a dowry.

The driver called out to the horses to stop. The metal wagon wheel rims squealed to a halt. The horses stomped their iron-shod feet on the cobbles and neighed.

The constable yanked me to my feet in the wagon bed. I tumbled off by way of the landing board, then looked up at the formidable bulk of the Hall of Justice. Torches blazed at its entrance. A tower in one corner made the building's shape remind me of my home, in a frightful, twisted way. The door was set deeply in the thickness of the stone walls. In the darkness it looked like a gaping mouth.

"Move along," the constable said, shoving my back. I stumbled, almost falling, and shuffled my way through the dark doorway.

The tunnel stretched long. We emerged in a shadowy foyer lined on every side with rough-hewn stone, with doorways leading off to tunnels in several directions. A pathetic glow came from two hanging iron chandeliers, each with only a few candle nubs apiece. Sounds bounced and echoed down the stone corridors: shouts, complaints, morbid laughter. Male voices, mostly, with an occasional caw that sounded female. With a shock I realized, these were the prisoners. Passing the time, unable to sleep. Someone bellowed a rude song until a chorus of voices protested. There were thumping sounds, and a groan.

Mother of God. Were they going to put me in there, alone and surrounded by criminals?

I heard a door shut. Looking up I saw that this foyer contained a wooden staircase leading to the second story and continuing upward into the tower. A bushy-mustachioed officer with large spectacles, dressed in a smart uniform, had exited a room on the second level and now stood leaning over a rail, watching us.

"What's this, then?" the officer on the landing above called down.

"Theft, Sergeant," the constable barked up. "This here young lady was caught in the public square, robbing the Crown Prince of a valuable gem, after dancing with him. Witnesses saw her, and she confessed to His Majesty, the king."

The sergeant on the landing above straightened. His graying mustache twitched. "Extraordinary." He descended the stairs.

The constable continued. "King Hubert says her case is to be overseen by Lord Coxley himself." An annoyed look passed the sergeant's face, but he suppressed it. He pulled a dingy book and pencil from a pocket and prepared to write.

"Who're your parents?" he demanded.

I would not oblige him by looking him in the eye.

"Dead."

"Names?"

"August and Olivia Chapdelaine." Immediately I wished I'd said nothing. I would die before I'd dishonor their names and memory. Now I'd simply die afterward. With a withering heart I considered that their names held no honor for anyone, tarnished as their reputations had become.

". . . Chap-de-laine," the sergeant murmured, apparently spelling it as he went. He finished and peered at me. The spectacles gave him a watery look. "Right. In that case, your parents being dead, who's your next of kin or party to be notified for the disposal of your remains?"

On the landing of the stairs stood a pile of moldering dust someone had neglected to sweep into the dustbins.

"Miss? Did you hear me? I said, 'Who's your—'"

"I heard you," I said. "There is no one to notify."

The sergeant made a grunt of irritation. "In that case we'll have to put a notice in the bulletins," he said, "to see if anyone steps forward to claim you."

To claim me. If no one wanted me living, who would claim me dead?

"Shall I put her in an overnight holding cell, sir?" the constable asked.

The sergeant shook his head. "All full of festival drunks and rowdies. Our little royal thief is in luck tonight. Lord Coxley's here, in his office." He gestured to the staircase behind him. "Had to sign off on a list of executions. But this takes priority. We'll tend to her case right now." He made a sweeping gesture with one arm, a mock display of gallantry. "Right this way, miss, if you'd be so kind." The constable, with a crude laugh, shoved me toward the stairs.

Waves of exhaustion fell over me as I lifted one weary leg after another to climb. I shook myself. Why now, when I needed every scrap of wits about me, when faced with my death, why did I want nothing more than a corner to fall down in and sleep?

The stairs wound on and on. Finally the climb ended at a small landing with a single door. Light crept out over the doorsill. The sergeant seemed to need to prepare himself to enter this sanctum. He wiggled his shoulders, threw out his chest, and brushed at his uniform before rapping on the door.

"Come in," called an indifferent voice.

The sergeant swallowed, then stepped inside. I followed.

The light inside the room blinded me. When my eyes adjusted, I found myself in an opulent office, quite unlike the dungeon atmosphere of the Hall of Justice. A vast Persian rug spread before me, and plush leather chairs dotted the room. Lamps gleamed on small tables, and a fire burned on a hearth behind a polished wooden desk. A lush bouquet of red roses stood on one corner of the desk, filling the room with suffocating sweetness.

Behind the desk, not yet looking up at us, sat a long, angular man, fastidiously dressed and poring over a stack of papers, a quill pen in one hand. He signed his name to a document, replaced the quill in its holder, and carefully blotted his signature. Then he placed the document aside, folded his immaculate fingers together, and raised his languid eyes to us.

The sergeant was nearly beside himself, waiting. When at last this Coxley graced us with his attention, the sergeant's tongue bolted like a racehorse out of its stall.

"Got a special case here, sir, sent by His Majesty himself! She—"

Coxley raised an imperious hand, silencing the sergeant without a glance. His attention was all on me.

He was younger than I'd have guessed, clearly not yet forty. Smooth-shaven face, thin blond hair combed to one side, clear and penetrating blue eyes. Handsome, I realized with surprise, in a cold, reptilian way. I stared, wondering if I'd ever seen him before, or if that was simply the effect of his powerful presence.

The trappings of civility all around his chamber might have made me hope his justice would be merciful, but there was something crystalline about him. Like glass, or ice. It chilled me. Though it surely meant death either way, I'd far rather trust my fate to the sergeant's mercies than his.

His eyebrows bowed slightly. "Who are you?"

There seemed to be no evading his questions. "Lucinda Chapdelaine."

"Ah." He nodded knowingly, as if his suspicions had been confirmed—as if he knew Lucinda Chapdelaine, and had an appointment with her two minutes hence.

"You've grown, I see. Naturally, you would."

This remark invited no reply, so I made none. What could he mean?

"How old are you?"

I ground my toe into a spot on the carpet. A weak display of defiance. "Fifteen."

He shook his head, like one toying with a small child. "Fifteen already? Where does the time go?" Condescension dripped like venom from his falsely smiling teeth.

"You speak as though you know me, and as though I should know you," I said stoutly.

He sneered. "Do you not?" He altered his voice to imitate a woman's. ". . . Lucy-lu?"

My breath caught in my throat. For an instant Mama was there, I could feel her, I could smell her. It was her voice that spoke. I hadn't heard it in ten years. My vision grew blurry at the edges.

Dear God, I'm going to cry, or faint. I closed my eyes and thought about breathing. Out. In. While I still could.

"What's the charge, Royer?" asked Coxley.

"Theft against the crown, sir," the sergeant said. He explained everything and added, "His Majesty says you're to handle her case personally."

Coxley began to laugh, a long, cruel noise that rumbled deep in his throat.

"Precious!" he said. "Simply brilliant."

Sergeant Royer and I exchanged a glance. In the presence of this enigma, even he and I became allies of sorts. Who was this snake, and how did he know so much?

Coxley's laugh ended. "Leave us," he said to Royer. "Untie the girl first."

The sergeant ripped the cords off my wrists and left without a sound.

Being untied should have been good news. Instead I felt like a mouse trapped by a cat who wanted to play first before eating me.

While Coxley kept his malevolent gaze trained on me, I looked around the room. No windows. No exit but the door behind me, which the sergeant pulled shut.

My only hope was the man behind the desk. I rubbed my aching arms. I would place no hope in him. That was what he wanted me to do, and I'd give him no such satisfaction. Hot anger welled up inside of me.

The pretend laughter vanished from Coxley's face.

"Where did you get those clothes?" he demanded.

Of all the questions he might ask, why this one? How could my clothes possibly matter?

I matched his gaze, or tried to. "Someone gave them to me."

His piercing eyes dared me to stare back. He doesn't blink, I realized with a start. At all.

"Who gave you access to your mother's things?"

How could he possibly know about my mother's things? Even if he'd known her, what kind of man remembered a dress after ten years?

Beryl. If I told him about Beryl, would he contact her? Would she come to my aid? Or would I be luring her into a trap?

"Who gave you access to your mother's things?" The razor's edge in his voice told me he wasn't used to being ignored.

Not even the king had such an air of power as this man—power that had nothing to do with yellow epaulets and gold chains.

Nevertheless, I thought, staring into his snake eyes, I do not have to answer him.

He shifted in his chair. "Are you acquainted with the woman called the Amaranth Witch?"

He knew about Beryl.

Reveal nothing with your face. Neither ignorance nor surprise. Though this man be the devil himself, tell him nothing.

He shifted slightly in his chair. Clearly determined not to let my composure exceed his own, he was a picture of calm detachment, but I knew I had unsettled him.

The clock ticked. The fire snapped. The roses gushed.

"What did you steal from the prince?"

I trained my thoughts on Mama, Papa, and home; on Beryl, and the home she yearned for.

"Miss Chapdelaine, it will go better for you if you cooperate with me. I have the power to oversee your sentencing. Did you know that?"

Red roses. Red flowers. Love-lies-bleeding. It does tonight.

"Royer!"

I head the door open behind me. It jolted me back to this place and moment.

"What did the prisoner take from the prince?"

The prisoner, ropes or not.

"Rare jewel, sir. Quite large, so Cuthbert tells me."

"Did Cuthbert see its color?"

A pause. "White, I believe he said, sir."

A wolfish smile passed across Coxley's lips. He nodded. "You may go."

The door closed again.

It hit me. He knew about Beryl's stone.

Coxley's long white fingers drummed with excitement on the desk. "You have put on a pretty display of defiance, Miss Chapdelaine. Shades of your father, with much of your mother's spirit about you, too. But stubbornness will not avail you. Even in your silence, you have told me everything I need to know."

He was the someone Beryl had warned me about! Only Beryl never knew that Lord Coxley, head of Saint Sebastien's Hall of Justice, was the one searching for her stone.

He pulled a sheet of parchment from a drawer and dipped his quill in a reservoir of ink. With a well-controlled hand he wrote on the leaf. I waited while he finished, blotted his work, folded it, then turned a candle on its side to drip hot wax on the seal.

"You are in league with the woman called the Amaranth Witch, who occupies your parents' former home. In some way Prince Gregor obtained possession of her"— he waved a hand in the air—"magical stone. You dared to steal it from him. Alas, your effort was unsuccessful, and now here you stand before me"—he let a snicker escape— "the daughter of my former employer, convicted of capital theft, and sentenced to die by hanging at dawn." He smiled his serpentine smile, then shuffled together some papers as though finished with me. "Though waiting till dawn is a tiresome convention that I aim to see abolished in time."

His former employer? Papa?

Who could this man have been? Clearly not the gardener's helper.

"The lawyer." As I spoke it, I knew it was true.

"Hmm?" he said.

"You're the solicitor. The one Papa didn't like. The one who had oversight of all his papers and properties."

Suppressed surprise, then irritation flickered across his face.

"Your father trusted me implicitly," he said. "You were too young to know anything at all about his dealings with his associates."

"I know he didn't trust you," I insisted. "He was planning to dismiss you. I heard him say so to Mama."

His eyes narrowed. "How would you remember such a thing?" He relaxed. "As if it mattered. The worms have long since finished with your parents. And soon they shall with you."

He rose and reached out an arm to me.

"Come, Miss Chapdelaine. You've given me no end of pleasure for the evening. To see August and Olivia's brat swing from the gallows is a perfect finale to a job half-done. Chance has favored me with a way to finish my work." He almost shivered with pleasure. "And delivered into my hands the one thing I need most."

He steered me toward the door, for all the world as though leading me to a dance floor. "And now, let me introduce you to your chamber mates for the remainder of the evening."

I shrank back. How could there be yet more to fear? Only two hours ago I was in Prince Gregor's arms. From bliss, to this, in a moment.

What would happen to Beryl, with him knowing so much about her?

Coxley opened the door. The sergeant stood there, blinking at us.

"Take Miss Chapdelaine to the holding cell, Royer," Coxley said.

The sergeant produced a note with a seal ripped open. "Messenger just arrived from the palace," he said.

The palace!

Coxley reached for the paper. He noted its open seal with a dark look at Royer.

"It wasn't addressed to anyone in particular," Royer said innocently.

Coxley glanced at the note, then at me.

"Their Graces," he bit off the words, "King Hubert and Prince Gregor, have seen fit to bestow a favor upon you."

My heart raced. I couldn't conceal it. A pardon! Gregor loved me still, and that would save me. He'd never let me die! He knew there was a mistake.

Coxley, who had seemed annoyed by this intrusion, saw my reaction and smirked. "They send a special request on your behalf, that you be incarcerated in a private cell, for your protection and comfort while you await your execution."

That was all?

No. It couldn't be.

I looked to Royer to refute this travesty. His spectacled eyes showed no emotion.

It was so.

"Sweet dreams," Coxley said to me, then, to the constables, "Take her away." He retreated into his office and pulled the door shut.

Royer bound my wrists. I made no resistance. He took a torch from the wall and led me down the stairs. I followed dumbly, unable to see in the dark through my tears.

Oh, I'd made an impression on the prince, all right. Better had he forgotten me utterly than send me this cruel half kindness, this private passage on my way to death.

At the bottom of both flights, Royer led me down a corridor to its end, past barred doorways from which the snores and groans of uncomfortable sleepers issued forth. He opened the last door on the left with an evil-looking key, and gestured me into a narrow cell, not wide enough for two people to stand abreast. There was one small window and a rough wooden bench. Little more than a stone coffin standing on end.

The door clicked shut behind him. I watched, wishing even he wouldn't leave me alone. His face appeared once more, making the lock fast. His brief glance my way held only resignation and indifference.

I stumbled backward until the wooden bench tripped me, and sat heavily upon it, smacking the back of my head against the rock. Numbness engulfed my skull.

Numbness was welcome.

Chapter 18

I huddled on the wooden bench all through the scant hours that remained, rubbing my prickly arms and legs and rocking on my hips. I am alive now, I told myself. I must savor it, even in this cold, rat-infested place, for I, Lucinda Chapdelaine, am alive. I am not dead. Yet.

Only the people I'd loved were dead. Papa, proud and clever Papa, snuffed out in his prime; and Mama, whose laughing eyes saw into my thoughts; and Uncle Ernest, poor old browbeaten Uncle Ernest, who saved me tidbits of dinner when Aunt was in a rage.

All those I'd loved were gone. If Prince Gregor had cared for me, even for a moment, he was wise to abandon it, for caring for me could bring nothing but ill luck.

Gregor. He was a bitter taste in my mouth, the sourness left after sugar ferments on the tongue. They were wrong, those who babbled that it was better to have loved and lost. I wished I'd never seen him.

Didn't I?

What had I done to end up like this? It was Beryl who dropped that accursed gem into my lap. Aunt who made me carry it back. Peter who stole it from me, and Beryl once more who sent me to retrieve it.

The sky through the bars of my window turned from black to pewter gray.

I am not dead.

I am not to blame.

If I was not to blame, then why was I in prison?

No one robbed the prince but I. No one plotted to do it but I. I chose it, I planned it, and I did it. No one else can claim that distinction but me!

I ceased my rocking and digested this information. It was strangely exhilarating. I was to blame. I was audacious! Determined! Resourceful! I did an unspeakable thing, myself, alone!

I jumped up off my bench, heedless of the damp chill of the flagstone floor.

I was a marvel of ingenuity and nerve. If I'd been one yesterday, surely I could be one now. I did it! They're going to hang me for it. But first they'll have to make me hold still long enough to tie the rope. And I've got talents they don't know of. Maybe those talents can save me.

I climbed onto the bench and stood on tiptoe to see if

the window held any possibilities. Its iron bars were closely spaced and crisscrossed into a grate. I was able to poke my fingers through—there was no glass—but they didn't budge a bit. There was no wooden casement, only bars sunk deep into the mortar and rocks on every side. Undaunted, I grasped every bar and tried with all my strength to rattle it, to find some give to it, like a child examining her mouth for a loose baby tooth.

Sure as Gibraltar, all of them.

Another way, then. I hopped down and hurried to the door. The silvery sky afforded me enough glow to see the knob. I rattled it, finding more satisfaction as it made a splendid racket.

"Shut up!" came a croak from across the way.

That wouldn't do. No sense in alerting the whole prison to my plan.

Time was fading. I crawled on hands and knees around my cell, combing across the floor with my fingers, in search of something that might help—a fragment of stone or metal, maybe, that could be used to aggravate the lock. But the floors held only dirt. No success.

I went back to the window and clutched the bars once more. So sweet, that moment's elation, letting me believe that with pluck alone I might steer events my way. It ebbed as quickly as it had come, leaving me full of nausea and dread.

Something warm and wet seized my fingers. I nearly fell backward off the bench.

"*Meh-heh-heh*," said a voice.

"Dog!"

He nuzzled my fingers affectionately, only biting them once or twice. He bit something on the ground and shoved it through the bars at me. It fell with a soggy plop on my upturned face and bounced onto the bench below me.

I stooped to pick it up. It was an apple, spongy and wrinkly, that he'd found goodness knew where, dripping with his saliva.

Bless his loyal heart. He'd brought me my last meal. I ate it.

"Thank you, Dog," I said between bites. "However did you find me?"

"*Meh-heh*," he said.

"I don't suppose you could fetch me a file, or some other bit of metal, could you? Something to pick a lock?"

"*Meh-heh-heh.*"

My words buzzed in my head. Something to pick a lock.

"Dog," I cried, "where's Peter? Can you bring me Peter?"

I begged a goat to bring me a rescuer. Desperate times leave no room for dignity.

"Peter, Dog," I cajoled. "Find Peter."

In answer, he leaned the whole wiry, hairy weight of his body against the grate, crushing my fingers between the cold metal and his warm hide.

"I love you, too, Dog," I said, and let my tears fall. We both knew Peter wouldn't come.

We stayed there for a while, watching the sky grow lighter. Surely they'd be coming soon. Dawn was practically here. Nothing but a miracle could save me now. If they must kill me, couldn't they do it now and spare me the dread of waiting? That would be just like one of Coxley's tricks, to promise execution at daybreak, then delay to prolong the torment.

Stirrings of morning were beginning to sound in the corridor. A voice called an insult to a cellmate. Another voice answered. From farther away came a voice telling the prisoners to shut their mouths.

I could begin to make out the cobblestones of the street, and the shuttered shops across the way. My time was short.

"Go, Dog," I said, shoving him with my fingers as best I could. "Hurry and go, before Coxley roasts you for dinner."

He shoved back at me and refused to budge. I prodded him harder, using my nails. "Go, you stubborn goat, for your own good! You can't help me now."

Footsteps and jingling keys sounded in the corridor.

My bowels turned to water. They were coming. Fear? From where I stood fear seemed a luxury.

I yanked my fingers free and hissed to Dog to go away, then turned.

The keys rattled in the lock. I saw Cuthbert, the

constable who'd arrested me and brought me here, through the hole in my door.

My breath came in gasps. Steady!

He opened the door and entered, holding a finger over his mouth, signaling me to be quiet. I wrapped my arms tightly around myself. He approached me and bent to whisper in my ear. His damp breath made me cringe.

"You want to live?"

I couldn't stop myself from nodding.

"Come with me, then, quiet as a fish, unless you're wondering how hanging feels."

Cuthbert, helping me escape? Was this a trick?

Did I dare question this chance?

I rose. He headed toward the door with a glance over his shoulder. I followed from a distance, my heart thumping. If he did intend to spare my life, what did he have in mind? Whatever it was, I could face it when it came.

I followed him through corridor after corridor, around labyrinthine turns and twists. As far as I could tell, we avoided the entrance hall entirely. Here in the depths of the great building the darkness pressed heavily upon me. The sleeping, muttering sounds of prisoners faded until the only sound was Cuthbert's boots on the stone.

The hallway ended with a wooden door. Cuthbert pulled a key from his pocket.

"She's out there, waiting for you," he said, wrestling with the stubborn lock.

"Who is?"

He eyed me sideways, as though I were a simpleton. "Your lady friend, the one that's bought your freedom."

Beryl. I began to tremble. How had she known? I wasn't alone after all. She'd saved me.

Cuthbert rattled the doorknob, and my anxiety rose. To be this close to freedom—*hallelujah!*—and still be impeded by a rusty lock was excruciating.

"Bought my freedom, you say?" I asked. "From Coxley, you mean? A pardon?"

He snorted. "You daft? Nobody buys a pardon from Coxley. Not little folk like you or me, leastways. No," he made the reluctant bolt spring back with a satisfying click. "She bought it from me." He jingled the coins in his pocket and showed his teeth. "Here's where I get the rest."

I shuddered. Thank heaven for a corrupt, underpaid constabulary.

He pulled the door open. Even the pale light of dawn was startling after the darkness. We were at a small door in the rear of the building, which abutted a narrow alleyway. The packed-dirt ground lay covered in frost, and a cold wind swept through the doorway.

"Get on with you, before I change my mind," he said. "She's waiting for you."

I stepped forward. The windowless bulk of the Hall of Justice loomed above, and on the other side, only a few feet away, another wall of stone rose, the rear of a building I did not know.

A hooded form appeared from behind some tall dust-bins and handed Cuthbert a small sack. He seized it, shook a few coins into his palm, nodded, then slammed the door violently, leaving me face-to-face with Beryl.

Except, it wasn't Beryl. The shape was wrong. She threw back her cloak.

It was Aunt.

Chapter 19

Her eyes were full of spite.

"You!" I said.

Was I going mad? Had they already executed me, and this was my delirium on the doorstep of hell?

"I'm sure we're both equally glad to see each other," she said. She seized my hand and slapped something into it. It pricked my palm.

"There," she said, turning to leave, "that settles things. I've done with you." She took off down the alleyway.

In my hand lay my rose-red bracelet, unrepaired, but clean. Sweet love of heaven.

I leaped after her and seized her arm.

She shook me off like I was a contagion.

I scurried to the other side of her so that I blocked her escape. I had to know.

"Why, Aunt?"

She scowled and made as if trying to get by me, but she didn't use all her force, as I knew too well. I planted myself firmly.

"I want to know why."

She looked up at the high bulk of the buildings on either side of us. Away from Uncle's shop, neither of us seemed to know what to do with each other.

"Them constables are going to be out here searching for you in a minute," she said. "You'd best run and ask no questions if you want to live."

She hurried off, disappearing down a connecting alley. I chased after her. She crossed a street, then darted into another alley. I caught her there and tugged her sleeve.

"Leave me be," she snapped.

"Where'd you get that gold?"

She stopped trying to get away. "You know where."

Beryl's gold, which she took from me last night. Unbelievable.

"But why did you do it?"

She glared at me. "You've been a pestilence and a vexation from the day Ernest brought you home. A spoiled little minx. A wedge in my marriage. A drain on my budget." Her bloodshot eyes burned. "I'll not have you as the ruination of my peace as well!"

I blinked. "I, the ruination of *your* peace?"

"Let me by," she said, almost pleading.

"Not until I understand," I said. "Why did you part with the gold when you hate me so?"

Aunt let out a long, troubled breath. She seemed to shrink as she did so. When she spoke, her voice was small, as if coming from far away.

"Last night Ernest came to me in a dream." She sniffled. "He said I'd betrayed my own." Her eyes flashed. "I don't call you my own."

She stood glowering at me, her chin quivering. Then, wonder of wonders, her face screwed up with—what? Grief? Remorse? Could it be possible?

"But Ernest called you his own," she said. "I thought I owed him this." She raked her sleeve across her eyes.

My voice broke on my words. "Thank you."

I knew I was speaking to Uncle, too.

She wouldn't look at me. For a moment her profile was that of a wide-eyed little girl with thick, dark curls.

She started briskly down the alleyway.

"Aunt!" I cried.

She stopped and turned, scowling back at me.

I swallowed my nervousness. I hadn't exactly planned what to say, nor even considered whether or not I ought to say it.

"Well?" she said.

"Thank you," I said again, this time with more feeling. "And . . . I'm sorry." She seemed taken aback. "For all that you've suffered. Not from me, but . . . Yes, from me, and from everything." I swallowed hard. "Things have been hard for you, and I know it. I'm just sorry about it, is all."

Aunt's face contorted into a grimace of bewildered disgust. She shook her head as if shaking me off like cobwebs, turned away, and disappeared down the alley.

Chapter 20

Aunt ran one way, and I, the other. Already I'd lingered too long near the Hall of Justice.

The sky grew lighter. Pale morning sun without warmth filtered down through the rooftops onto the dingy streets in this part of town.

My stomach rumbled, and my head ached. A sleepless night left me physically spent. To Beryl's, I supposed, I'd go, to admit defeat and beg a change of clothes before fleeing the country.

I paused for a moment's rest in another alley, sliding down the side of a building and sitting on the ground. Hardly any sunlight penetrated here. The darkness made me feel safer.

Clattering footsteps made me jump in terror. Before I could see who was coming, wet rubbery lips explored my face and a *meh-heh-heh* erupted in my ear. I wrapped my arms around Dog's neck and kissed his wiry cheek. He settled down beside me and let me pet him, lending me his precious warmth.

Street traffic increased in the stretch of road I could see at the mouth of the alley. Milk trucks and vegetable carts pulled by tired old horses passed in either direction. Hawkers' voices rose on the morning air. Walkers hurried by on their way to work or to market. Did they know how lucky they were to be about on the streets, with a warm coat and a belly full of breakfast and no constables to molest them?

In only minutes, I knew, my flight would be known, and Coxley would send his men to scour the surrounding areas for me. Would Cuthbert invent a story? How close would it come to the truth? Close enough to catch me? He had his gold now.

I knelt down, rubbing my hands in the dirt. I smeared it over my face, rubbing dirt into my hair and fouling it up with tangles. I tore at my clothing, ripping off any bits of lace or ribbon, so it looked tattered and spent. A disguise, of sorts. Half the city had seen me dance with the prince then be arrested. Or so it had seemed last night.

I fled the alley.

Every moment I expected to hear a shout, a whistle, a commotion signaling that someone had sounded the alarm. All I heard were surprised noises from people as I breezed by them. "What's your hurry?" "Where's the fire?" and such.

Perhaps I was attracting too much attention this way. I slowed until I reached a corner, ducked around it, and sped up again, only to collide head-on with someone.

He fell backward. I landed on top of him, smacking my forehead sharply against his jaw. It stung so badly I was sure the skin had cracked open. I winced in pain, afraid to open my eyes and see who I'd toppled. I tried to climb over him and stand up. Dog trod on him too.

The man seized both my wrists, and I collapsed bodily on top of him once more.

"Well, you're a mess," his voice said. "Fancy meeting you this morning."

Oh no.

I forced my eyes open. I shut them again.

It was Peter, grinning like a monkey.

I wrenched my hands loose from the hold he had on me and climbed to my feet, taking no pains to avoid stepping on him, and continued on my way. I'd not talk to that scoundrel for all the money in the world.

In a moment he was at my side, jogging comfortably and brushing the dirt off his jacket. I pressed on, determined to avoid him. But he was about as easy to lose as a barnacle.

"You've mussed up my hat," he said after a while.

"Blast your hat."

"And where are we off to?" he asked, sounding as though a picnic were planned.

"'We' aren't off to anyplace," I said. "I am off to wherever you're not."

"That's odd," he said. "I was on my way to find you."

Oh, indeed. "Ha."

"Was so," he said. "Though I certainly didn't expect to find you like this."

I glared at him.

He colored. "That is to say, er, you're looking well! Compared to . . . ahem."

"Compared to a corpse?" I snapped. "Forget it, Peter. Just forget it. And go away."

He closed his mouth for a blessed moment or two, but he didn't go away.

I halted and grabbed his sleeve. "What do you mean, you were 'looking for me'?"

He swallowed. From the looks of it, an entire potato. "I didn't want you to be alone out there," he said. "And afterward I was going to make sure you had, er, the right sort of burial." He jingled the contents of his pocket and grinned awkwardly. "Figured—seeing as now you're a customer—you had that coming to you. Was going to have them put satin in your coffin. Blue, I thought, would suit you."

A blue satin coffin.

Once, he'd amused me—in a maddening sort of way—with his audacity and wit. No more.

"Your loyalty to your customers is touching," I said. "I

should have known you'd only treat me decent if I was dead."

He looked stung. I was glad of it. I marched on. He didn't follow.

At first.

The sun was full up now. I ignored Peter and took stock of where I was. The road sloped gradually uphill, as so many thoroughfares in St. Sebastien did, toward the palace, which stood sentinel over the highest part of the city. Beyond it to the north lay the river, and then my parents' home, and after that the open countryside and the road that would take me, after several weeks' journey, out of Laurenz and into Hilarion, where perhaps I could begin a new life.

North. That's where I'd go.

Peter caught hold of my sleeve. Dog wedged himself protectively between me and Peter.

"How'd you get out, anyway?" he asked, admiration in his voice. "Did you escape?" He whistled. "What an adventure, eh?"

"Leave me alone."

The palace. Its towers of brown stone rose like stacks of buttered toast. I was so hungry I could have bitten it.

"Let me buy you breakfast," Peter said.

Peter, part with cash? My hollow belly squirmed. But I'd not be beholden to him.

"No."

Peter blocked my path. "Why're you so sour? I'm just trying to help."

It was a mistake, listening to him. He only made me furious. I could have ground my teeth to powder.

"You, help?" Here came the tears again. I squashed them back down furiously. He shall not, he shall *not* see me cry!

"You, help!" I repeated for good measure. "Help me out of a fortune, help me into prison, help me into the hangman's noose! Help me right into the paws of rogues and scoundrels! Next time why don't you just help me off a cliff and be done with it?"

I was shouting. I couldn't stop. Peter looked like he'd stepped outdoors to use the privy and found himself knee-deep in a flood.

I rushed on. "I could have died, Peter! Because of you! And they'll be out hunting for me any moment, and I may die yet. Because of you! Help, indeed. You only help yourself, to everything around you that catches your eye."

I thought I saw the first real glimmer of remorse in his crestfallen face then.

"I've been up all night feeling awful about you," he said.

Much good that had done me. This wasn't enough. "So?"

"If I'd known what would come of it, I wouldn't have stolen your gem."

An admirable but altogether unhelpful conclusion. If

I'd known what would have happened, I wouldn't have stolen it last night, either.

He looked me in the eye from underneath his curtain of dark hair. "I'm sorry."

"I should think you would be," I snapped, and stalked off.

This time he didn't follow.

I stopped.

I looked back. He hadn't moved from the spot where we'd been.

Lucinda, you're a fool to forgive him.

"Well, are you coming?" I called.

A grin lit his face. He closed the gap between in a second.

We looked at the awakening city. The streets were dirtier than usual, littered with yesterday's debris from the Winter Festival. Unlike the day before, the sky overhead was flat and gray with low-hanging clouds.

I kept the palace as my Polaris as we wended our way through ever more crowded streets. At least, I thought, festival crowding would conceal me from constables.

"Where are you bound?" Peter asked—a careful and cautious Peter.

"Bridge," I said. "Any one of them will do to get me where I'm headed."

Peter shook his head. "Any one of them will do for you to lose your head, you mean."

I bristled. "What do you mean, lose my head? I'm as rational as you are."

He shook his head urgently. "I mean, you daren't cross any bridges. You said they'd be looking for you? If that's so, they'll have officers posted at all of them by now, searching for you, and then back to jail you go."

It felt like a hand had seized my throat and started squeezing. I tried to fight back.

"They can't all know what I look like, can they?"

"Well enough," Peter said. "You've got the same clothes. I wouldn't want to be any girl trying to leave the city today. They'll investigate them all."

"But I have to reach Riverside," I said, panic flooding. "It's the only place I can hide."

As soon as I said it, I knew I was wrong. I couldn't hide there. Coxley knew I'd been to my parents' home, and it had confirmed his suspicions—that the home's new occupant and the Amaranth Witch were one person.

Now I had a new concern. I started running once more. "I have to get there to warn Beryl!"

"Who's Beryl?" Peter asked.

"The stone belongs to her," I explained between breaths. "She's the one who gave me the nice clothes I wore yesterday. They were my mother's, long ago."

Peter paused. "Your mother's?"

I elbowed past a woman carrying a tray of hot buns, and she spilled them. A stream of curses followed me. I stammered an apology and hurried on. When I looked back at Peter, he was eating a bun, and another was dangling from Dog's bearded mouth.

"Give me that!" I snatched the bun from Peter's hand and bit into it. He started to protest, then shrugged.

I finished the bun. "My father was a wealthy merchant before he died," I said between bites. "He and Mama and I used to live in one of the mansions on Riverside."

Peter whistled. "How'd you come to be scrubbing floors in a second-rate shop, then?"

I shook my head. "No time for that now. Point is, Beryl now lives in that mansion, and I've got to warn her that Coxley's after her."

"Unless I'm mistaken," Peter said, "he's after you. Over here!" Peter yanked me into a darkened doorway and halfway up a flight of stairs. A pair of constables on horseback cantered by. Dog stood guard and insulted their horses.

We hid in the stairwell until city noises swallowed the hoofbeats. Then Peter ventured down the stairs. I grabbed his sleeve and pulled him back into the shadows.

"Peter," I said, "you've been a criminal your whole life. It's a little new to me. How do I reach the river and cross it without getting caught?"

He pursed his lips. "For starters, there's disguise, but you're already a sight different from yesterday. As for the river, I know a fellow with a boat who might help us out if the price was right." I started to speak but he silenced me. "This one's on me. I owed you a coffin anyhow."

We ventured down the stairs and into the street.

"As for getting through the city without getting caught,"

Peter went on, "I always say, go to where they'd least expect to find you."

Where they'd least expect to find me.

I scarcely knew where I'd expect to find me.

I looked around for inspiration. Of course! I snapped my fingers. "That's it."

"What's it?"

"You've given me the answer," I said. "It makes perfect sense."

"Oh?"

"I may not survive this night, Peter. I've got one chance left. Besides, there's someone I need to see." I swallowed.

Could I? Yes, I could face him now. Calm as sunrise.

Peter scratched his head. "Pardon my saying so, but you've lost your wits in jail. It happens. Torture."

"Be still. Come on, we're almost there." Somehow I found new strength. I began to run.

"Where?"

I pointed straight ahead, to the rippling flags on the towers and entryways of Sebastien Palace, a quarter of a mile away.

Peter stopped short. "That's carrying advice a bit far, don't you think?"

"Not at all," I panted. "I need to see the prince."

"Well, what are you going to do, knock on the front door and ask for him?"

I considered. "More or less. He holds court, doesn't he?"

"The king does, and sometimes the prince assists him. Not likely today, though. Festival. Impending wedding."

I ran on, wiping my sweating face on the sleeve of my dress.

"I'll talk my way in. I'll tell them it's urgent."

"No, you won't," Peter said. "You'll come with me." He grabbed my arm and pulled me down a narrow covered path leading away from the palace entrance.

I pushed at his arm to no avail. "Where are you taking me?"

"Trust me."

A fat lot of good that had done me in the past. I swallowed a rude remark.

The path wound about like a tunnel in a cave, lit only by sunlight through occasional breaks in the ceiling. I felt hemmed in. At last we came to a wooden door. Peter pulled a ring from his pocket containing keys and key picks and had the door open in seconds.

He glanced down at Dog, one hand on the doorknob.

"He can't come in here," he said.

I knelt and scratched Dog's ears. "Stay here, now, boy, understand?" He grunted at me but didn't protest when we closed the door behind us.

"Not a sound, now," Peter whispered, and gestured for me to follow him.

We emerged into a frozen winter garden, on a path overhung by hydrangea branches. Their leaves had fallen but a few withered blossoms still clung. Small statues of squirrels and rabbits dotted the stone path. A peaceful, almost reverent feeling hung over the place. The high wall and trees held the city's noises at bay.

It was so enchanting I lost sight of myself for a moment. "Hurry," Peter whispered, startling me out of my reverie.

The hydrangeas thinned, and Peter walked more stealthily, pausing between steps. Once he stood stock-still for a minute, and I wondered why, until he pointed at a retreating figure roving through the gardens. He's a palace guard, I told my thumping heart, not a city constable.

Peter gestured, and we scurried over a walkway paved with white pebbles and lined with bare, dignified trees, until we came to the rear castle walls. Above us hung the curved bottom of a stone balcony. We crouched, half-hidden in evergreen shrubbery below.

Peter picked up a pebble from the walk and tossed it onto the balcony above us.

We waited.

He tossed another pebble. I heard it *ping* on the balcony floor. It echoed across the frosty gardens.

"Must be he's gone," I whispered.

"Dead asleep, more like," Peter said.

I pictured Prince Gregor asleep, and then I pictured him awake, coming into the shop, and dancing with me twice. My courage melted. Filthy clothes, dirty face and hands, what was I thinking?

"Peter," I said, "maybe this isn't . . ."

He launched a fistful of pebbles into the sky. They landed on the balcony about as quietly as a vase smashing.

". . . such a good idea," I finished lamely.

A door opened.

Footfalls shuffled.

A pebble landed on the walk, followed by half a dozen more. I covered my head with my arms.

A sleep-thick voice floated downward. "This had better be important, Peter."

Chapter 21

Gregor leaned over the railing, rubbing his eyes with the backs of his hands. His hair dangled below his chin, dark with a night's whiskers.

"Well? You coming up?"

He finished rubbing his eyes and blinked at us.

"There's two of you," he observed. "Who's the . . . Oh."

I had risen.

"Peter," Gregor said slowly, not taking his stern eyes off me, "what is going on here?"

Oh, I can face him now, calm as sunrise. Sunrise through a hurricane.

"I must speak with you," I said. My voice squeaked.

Gregor's eyes were full of pain. "How are you not in prison?" he asked quietly.

"Conversations like these," Peter interrupted, to my great relief, "are better off face-to-face. Upsy-daisy." He crouched before me, offering his knee as a stool for me so I could clamber over the railing. Oh, let me do this gracefully, I prayed. Let me not fall on my face. Not today.

I stood on Peter's leg and reached the ledge. Gregor hesitated, then reached his hands out and swung me onto the balcony. A moment later Peter had climbed up.

Gregor gestured us inside. Peter flopped onto an embroidered couch near the fireplace. I stood by the fire, taking in the plush and polished furniture, the rugs, the flowers, the tapestries, the bed. I felt like a chimney sweep in a linen shop. Just brushing against something I would pollute it. I shivered as the fire showed me how cold I'd been.

Gregor pulled the door shut, drew his curtains, and turned to face us both. His face turned in an instant from weariness to fury.

"How *dare* you two show up here?"

I was so startled I stepped back, bumping into the mantel.

Peter took a good-humored approach. "I know it's early," he said, "and we didn't exactly have an invitation . . ."

"How dare you show up here after trying to rob me last night?"

I felt sick to my stomach anew.

"*I* didn't try to rob you," Peter pointed out in a hurry. "*She* did."

Curse you, Peter.

Gregor looked at me. "A thief in training," he said in a

low voice, shaking his head. It took all my self-possession not to cry.

"You work together, don't you?" Gregor said, striding around the room but glaring at Peter. "When her attempt failed, you thought you'd have another go, did you? Anyway, I don't mean that time. *She* spent the night in prison for it. Where were *you* all night?"

Peter looked like a bug pinned to a paper. "Hanging around the Hall of Justice for a bit, then back home," he said. "God's truth."

"Watch yourself," Gregor said. "Don't blaspheme."

"Prince Gregor," I burst out, "what are you talking about?"

He looked back at me, and again, his anger turned to hurt. "Two hours ago, I left my bedroom for a moment, and I was waylaid by *someone*," he bit off the word. "A *man*"—he stared accusingly at Peter—"dressed in a mask and dark clothing." He frowned and rubbed his chin. "No, I suppose it can't have been you, Peter," he said. "This man was extraordinarily strong."

Peter puffed out his chest.

"This person clamped his hand over my mouth and searched my person. He didn't find what he was looking for. He demanded I tell him where the stone was." Gregor was livid. "I fought him off the best I could, but he ... at any rate, he took off running faster than I could give chase. And when I called my guards, they were nowhere near."

He turned back to face me. "Did you send someone to steal it back from me?"

Coxley.

"I swear that I did not, Your Highness," I said. I prayed my sincerity showed plainly. I itched to say, "I know who did!" But how could I ever prove it?

Gregor's gaze riveted me to the mantelpiece.

I looked back at him, watching his blue eyes.

At last he nodded slowly. "I believe you, Miss Chapdelaine," he said.

This time my eyes filled with tears. I blinked them away. There was no reason why he should believe me.

Gregor sat down on a chair. He looked exhausted. He raked his hands over his face and hair as if in utter despair. "If you haven't come to confess, then why have you come?"

I took a deep breath, and then another. Reaching a hand into my pocket, my fingers found the remains of my childhood charm bracelet. I seized it and stroked it. It gave me courage.

"I'm sorry to disturb you." I took another breath. "I know the hour's early, but I had to be up early, because" — Gregor's gaze was unnerving — "that's when they were going to kill me."

He looked away.

"How did you escape?" he asked. "Did they set you free?"

I swallowed. Would he call Rolf and send me back?

"A . . . a friend helped me. More than that, I cannot say." I licked my lips. "I know you could send me back to jail, and you'd be justified. But I hoped . . . I trusted in your kindness"—the prince shut his eyes—"and dared to come and explain myself, and explain whose the stone is." I took a deep breath. "And why I need it back."

He opened his eyes with apparent effort.

"You thought, I was a fool for you last night, perhaps I would be again?"

Peter let out a low whistle. I was stung with shame.

"Who *are* you?" Prince Gregor asked. "No pretenses. I need to know."

It was good that he needed to know. Good that he needed anything from me.

I stood a little taller. "I am Lucinda Chapdelaine," I said. "Daughter of August and Olivia Chapdelaine. You were right when you said you thought you'd known me from your childhood. Our parents were intimates, and we were children together. I remember you."

He studied my face for an uncomfortably long time. Then I could tell that he remembered, if vaguely.

He rubbed his head again.

"Yes. Then . . . why the goldsmith's shop?"

I rubbed my little red rose until I feared the enamel would fall off. "My parents died when I was five, and their wealth was stolen from me," I said. "My uncle by marriage, the goldsmith, was the only one who wanted me once it was plain I would be no heiress. But his second wife hated me. And there I've lived for the past ten years, until his death, when my aunt kicked me out."

"She was the woman who accused you?" he asked.

I nodded.

"An unpleasant person." He rose from his chair and paced, still keeping a safe distance from me. "So, you robbed me because of poverty."

"*No!*" I reigned in my voice with an effort. "No. Never that." Regret settled over me. "I have never taken anything from anyone in the world, until last night."

"You picked a fine time to start," Gregor said, his voice a lash. "What was I, some challenge? The start of a new career?" The bitterness he'd restrained until now startled me.

"No!"

He was hurt, and it was I, the scrubber of floors, who had wounded him!

Standing so near the fire toasted my backside. I moved closer to him.

"I had to get the stone back because it belonged to me! No. Not to me, but it was entrusted to me by someone. I had to get it back to that person."

Gregor frowned. "It was mine. I paid three thousand for it."

He didn't understand. "Don't you see?" I said. "You bought it from Peter! He stole it from me!"

Our heads turned in Peter's direction. He'd been lounging, apparently enjoying the show, but at this turn of events he scuttled to the end of the couch like an escaping spider. Now caught, his eyes darted back and forth between us.

"She can't prove that," he said. "No warranties, no refunds."

I stamped my foot. "How dare you deny it, Peter! D'you think I came here to discuss horse racing? I've come to set things right, and to get my stone! Do the right thing for once in your scheming life and tell the truth!" I regained my breath. "And give Gregor back his money."

Peter folded his arms and sat like a clam, his eyes shooting daggers at me. More the fool I, for thinking his timid overtures this morning meant he was my repentant, loyal friend.

Gregor's face, taking all this in, betrayed no emotion.

I hadn't come this far to let Peter forfeit the game. If he wouldn't give the money back, there was nothing left for me but to beg.

I approached Gregor and went down on both knees before him.

"Please," I said. "To you the stone is an exotic gem. A gift for your bride. It could be replaced by almost anything. To its owner, its significance is far greater. It has . . ." I needed to tread carefully here, lest they send me to a madhouse this time. "It has a power, of sorts, a connection to her soul that is irreplaceable." Still his face gave me no sign if my words were penetrating his scorn. "And for me," I continued helplessly, looking at his slippers, "it means— or meant—everything."

Gregor gestured for me to rise again. "How so, Miss Chapdelaine?"

Not my given name. Not Lucinda.

I took a deep breath. "Its owner had the means of restoring to me my name and some portion of my birthright, which I lost when my parents died." I felt naked, groveling, saying these words. "It would have meant the end of my dependency upon others."

"Not anymore?"

Oh, the gentle voice. I felt a lump in my throat. But I thought of Coxley. There was no place for me in a world where he held power. "The way things have transpired, I'm afraid not."

My merry dancing partner from last night now sat as grave and sober as a judge. A good one, too, I thought with a broken heart. That air of pure goodness about him that I'd felt the first time I saw him was even stronger now. This would be easier if I could hate him later.

He stood and walked to the mantel. I clutched my bracelet in my pocket, fingering the clasp Uncle never fixed.

"Sorrows all around in the way things have transpired," Gregor said. He opened a jade box and removed Beryl's stone. At the sight of it a tingle ran up my back.

"Do you know, Miss Chapdelaine, that I bought this stone off of our light-fingered friend there with the thought of presenting it to my future wife, the princess Beatrix. But as soon as I held it in my hands—and met her, soon after— I felt she was not its rightful owner. I couldn't make sense of it. It was almost as if the stone had a will of its own."

If only you knew. I waited, my heart thumping.

"I puzzled over it. I became so absorbed in the mystery that I carried it around with me, thinking perhaps it might tell me whose it was."

Again he rubbed the exhaustion from his eyes.

"The curious thing, Miss Chapdelaine, is that when I danced with you last night, I had the strongest sensation I should give it to you. It never occurred to me that it might have been yours to begin with."

Once more his gaze compelled me to look back, no matter how much I'd rather not. I stroked the bracelet, tiny between my finger pads. Here was a knot where the chain had kinked.

Here were the broken ends of my chain.

"I asked you to come to the ball tonight so I could give it to you myself." He laughed, a short, unconvincing sound. "A wild thought, I suppose. But the music, and the dancing, put wild thoughts into my head. Such as breaking off my betrothal to Princess Beatrix. A monumental task that would have been! My mother, my father, the king and queen of Hilarion, with all their court here visiting . . . but last night, with the music playing, I actually thought I'd do it."

My eyes flooded and I turned away. His elegant quarters disappeared behind tears. Just as well; I couldn't bear to face him. Yet an accusation buzzed in my head, demanding to be said.

"You felt all this, yet you sent me to my death willingly enough," I said. Sobbed.

There was a long silence. I closed my eyes.

"Was it I who sent you?" His voice wavered.

He was crying!

No less was I. But I couldn't stop stabbing yet.

"You lost no sleep over it," I said. "You slept like a baby. Peter had to wake you."

I felt petty and foolish, my bitterness spent. I rubbed my eyes and waited.

"You're mistaken, Miss Chapdelaine," Gregor said. He brushed a finger against my chin, asking me to look at him in the eye. What I saw there was a wide, gentle patience, calm like Laurenz Harbor on a summer morning, and forgiving. I hated to need his forgiveness. But I had no power to blame him when I looked him in the face.

I watched his lips as he spoke. "I haven't slept at all this night. I wasn't asleep when Peter summoned." He gestured with one hand toward a room that adjoined this one. A private chapel. A small nave, with an altar for kneeling. Dozens of candles flickered against the walls.

"I was praying."

+ + +

He waited a few minutes for me to compose myself. He then took my wrist and placed the stone in the palm of my hand.

"I give this to you now," he said, "because clearly it belongs to you. Peter can owe me. I'll write to Lord Coxley and issue you a full pardon, and I'll summon a carriage to escort you safely to wherever you wish. I imagine Coxley's hounds are out in full force by now."

I clenched the stone in my fist. Having it back brought no relief, no joy. No more did my pardon. Kindnesses from Gregor were worse than blows now.

"One thing more, Miss Chapdelaine. I must rescind my invitation to the ball tonight," he said, his voice gravelly and strange. "The night is devoted to presenting Princess Beatrix, the future queen of Laurenz, to her people. I must remember my duty to her, and to them." His eyes bored holes through me. "And in the future, I'll remember not to heed rash ideas that arise when dancing with pretty girls."

He spared me the faintest sliver of a wry smile, which somehow I returned, shattered though I felt. Yes, sweet. I remembered our moments together, too, and always would.

No less than this one.

Chapter 22

Ragamuffins such as I did not often ride in the prince's personal carriage. I didn't need the footman's sneer to tell me so. He shut my door, sparing me a brief glance of reproach, as though I might muddy its upholstery.

"Will you look at that?"

Peter made no attempt to conceal his admiration. He slid back and forth over the polished leather seat, and picked at the ornaments on its lanterns.

The horses started abruptly, and both of us were thrown back against the stiff cushions. Beryl's gem slipped from my fingers and fell to the floor. Peter pounced on it.

"I'll take that," I said, holding out my hand.

"Half a second," he said, holding it up to his eye.

I snatched it forcibly from his hand. "I said I'll take that."

"Criminy," Peter said, rubbing his palm, "you don't

think I'd steal that thing again, do you? After all the trouble it's caused?"

"In a heartbeat," I replied. "Or less."

I watched the city sweep by through the windows. Even with festival traffic, the royal coach had no trouble getting through. Everywhere we went faces turned to stare, in hopes of seeing Prince Gregor, no doubt. Imagine their confusion at seeing ragtag me instead. I sat back and pulled down the blinds.

The carriage's movement made me uneasy. I sat small in a corner of the seat opposite Peter and clutched the gem close to my heart with both hands. It thrummed reassuringly. I itched to escape the carriage. The inside smelled of fur and perfume and mint.

I'd ridden in carriages like this one as a child, but never since my arrival at Aunt's. And not only because there was no money to hire them. I feared them. Mama and Papa had died when their carriage tipped into a ravine on their way home from the ball that night.

And Coxley had been the one in charge of things as soon as my parents were gone. The one who sent away the servants and sold off so many of my parents' valuables.

He was the same man who took such delight in sending me to my death.

What had he said, about his unfinished work? And watching me die would conclude it? Last night those words had slid underneath other, more urgent fears. Now they demanded attention.

Had he murdered my parents?

Could such a question ever be answered after so many years?

Hadn't he all but admitted it?

The answer was present in the asking. Of course he had. I was sure of it. He would, and he did. I knew it. It was as though the whole universe had been poised, holding its breath, waiting for me to make this discovery.

He'd been an upstart working for my father ten years ago, and now he was the second most powerful man in the kingdom. *Lord* Coxley. The king's arm of justice. Such transformations took fortunes. Among other things.

Ruthless enough to do it, clever enough to conceal it, shrewd enough to profit from it.

I felt numb. Empty, as though I'd drained out of myself. That my parents had died in a tragic accident was my life's central truth. This horror was paralyzing—not mere chance, but deliberate evil had stolen them from me.

They'd been killed. Their killer was determined to finish the task of exterminating my family. And I'd just slipped through his fingers. He was not one to take that lightly.

We crossed the bridge without incident, despite a cluster of constables waiting at the toll booth. Gregor's carriage, it seemed, was not subject to searching.

"This is the life for me," Peter said, folding his arms

behind his head. "Snap your fingers and you're at the head of every line, and no nosy officers. Do what you want, when you want!"

I shook my head. "I don't think Prince Gregor sees it that way. It's not just a life of ease."

Before long we drew close to the fork in the lane where the road led off to my—Beryl's—house. I rapped on the window, and the driver reined in the horses.

"Would you let us off here, please?" I called.

The footman opened the door and helped me down with the least possible civility. Peter jumped down, muttering that I should have let them drive us all the way.

"What do you mean, 'us'?" I asked between my teeth, watching the carriage circle around and head back. "I don't know where you think you're going."

"Why, to visit you, of course," he said, "and pay my respects to this Beryl of yours."

I gave up. If I didn't let him in the door, he'd come in through a window.

"This way," I said, trudging off.

We reached the lawns. Peter whistled. "This is where you grew up?"

Was it? "Just till I was five."

Peter laughed. "You would have been a catch after all! Even for His Royal Blue Eyes."

I rubbed dust kicked up by a carriage wheel out of my eye.

We rounded the curve in the drive and the house came into view. Even with a bleached sun hiding behind curtains of cloud cover, and bare trees clawing the sky, and frozen, shriveled shrubbery, it was magnificent.

Peter shook his head. "You had all this and lost it?" I thought I saw real sympathy in his eyes. "I'm going to be a lot nicer to you from now on."

I laughed.

"And anyway, you might get it all back, right?"

Then I really laughed. It felt good to laugh. What else could I do?

I wiped my eyes and looked up to see Dog barreling toward me from behind the house. How on earth? I dropped down on my knees and embraced him. He nuzzled my face.

"*Faugh*," Peter groaned, grimacing and looking away.

"How'd you get here, Doggy Goat?" I asked, stroking his ribs. "How'd you pay your toll to cross the river?"

He eyed me from one side—as he must, being a goat—and butted me gently.

"I'm sorry, Dog. We left you at the palace, didn't we?"

"*Meh-heh-heh.*"

"Such a clever goat as you. You didn't mind, did you?"

I looked up to see Peter rolling his eyes.

"When you're done with your little love affair, can we go inside? I'm famished."

I climbed to my feet. "Come on, then. But you're not likely to find a meal here."

We headed down the walk toward the front door, but Dog would have none of it. He sidled against me and leaned hard, pushing me onto the lawns until I nearly fell.

"What's the matter, Dog? We want to go inside."

He was adamant. He pushed me, tripped me, and each time I persisted in ascending the walkway. Finally he galloped a few steps ahead of me and braced himself, his horns lowered.

"Your little puppy plans to ram you, I think," Peter observed.

I was astonished. "I believe you're right." Dog and I faced each other for a tense moment, until finally I stepped off the path and began strolling across the grass in the direction he'd been pushing me. He trotted over and fell into step at my ankles.

Peter shrugged and followed us as we cut a circle around the house. Who knew what obscure fear had entered his goat brain and possessed him to steer me away from the door? And what harm would it do to oblige him?

When we'd reached the back he herded us against the wall of the house, where, if we craned our necks around some statuary of a Greek god—which, in the presence of Peter, made me blush a bit—we could just get a glimpse through the tall windows overlooking the terrace. Without thinking I slipped a hand into my pocket and felt for Beryl's gem. It was practically humming with agitation.

Dog *maaahed* over and over, loud and agitated. I looked around, bewildered, trying to find some reason for his strange behavior. He kept up his racket without cease. Peter swatted his hide with his hat—not roughly, or I'd have returned the favor.

A movement caught my eye. Coming the other way around the rear of the house, walking cautiously, was Beryl.

She saw me. She hitched up her skirts and ran to me, seizing me in a tight embrace.

"You're back," she said in my ear. "You're back."

Chapter 23

I staggered back on clumsy feet. She steadied me effortlessly, her smile beaming. "I've been so worried about you," she said, rubbing my arms up and down as if searching for broken bones. "Are you all right? You look as though you've been through a terrible fright."

And that was when I dissolved into sobs. Beryl held me in her arms and rubbed my back.

Peter, ever helpful, offered Beryl an explanation.

"Girls are always going off in hysterics, but this time she's got cause," he said. "Nearly got hung, spent the night in jail, they probably intimidated her something fierce there. Made a strumpet of herself last night, on account of her shameless dancing with the prince, and then doesn't she get hauled off and arrested for robbing him."

With each accusation, Beryl made soothing noises, until I pulled myself off her shoulder.

"Peter, will you shut your mouth?" I cried. "Nobody asked you anything!"

Beryl looked like she was keeping her face straight only with great effort. She held a hand out to Peter. "I'm Beryl," she said. "I understand you're a common street thief?"

Peter bristled. "Hardly a common one."

Beryl demurred. "I stand corrected."

I pulled Beryl's gemstone from my pocket. It shimmered, pink and jubilant.

Her face was full of emotion as she took it from my hand. "Well done, Lucinda," she said. "Well done. I thank you."

Peter's eyes, I saw, had followed this transaction longingly.

"Keep it away from him," I warned. "He could rob the Holy Father of his underdrawers."

"Hey!"

"You're the reason for all this trouble in the first place," I reminded him. I turned to Beryl. "You're mistaken," I told her. "It wasn't well done. It was as poorly done as it could possibly have been. Everything I could ruin in the process, I did."

She regarded me cryptically. "Most things are harder to ruin than you think." She smiled and held out her arms, gesturing with a sweep toward the house and all the grounds. "I give you, Lucinda, your house, once more. Welcome home."

My legs felt weak. *I did it!* But I didn't. Or, I had no

chance of keeping it. The house felt no more mine than Sebastien Palace. I waved away these thoughts, remembering Beryl creeping around the hedge.

"What are you doing outside, Beryl?" I asked. "Were you hiding?"

She looked around surreptitiously, then shepherded us both toward a rear door to the house. "Come inside, quickly," she said. "I don't dare stay here long. There isn't much time."

We went inside and collapsed on couches in the parlor. Beryl got to work pulling paintings down from the walls. First the smiling youth, and then Aunt as a young girl. She wrapped them in soft cloth, then tied them with string. Then she sat and took my hands in hers.

"A man was here, just now. He came and searched the house," she said in an urgent whisper. "That's why I was outdoors. I decided I'd rather spy on my enemy than confront him. It's *him*! The man who's been trying to steal my stone. I got a better look at him. He only just left. It's a wonder he didn't see you. If you'd gone in the front door, he might have."

"Lucinda's goat wouldn't let us," Peter said.

I sat up straight. "Beryl, was he tall, with pale hair and blue eyes?"

Beryl nodded. "And an official uniform, with epaulets."

"That's him!" I cried. "It's Lord Coxley, the king's Chief Minister of Justice."

She sank back, clutching at her hair. "Of course. Of course! Why didn't I see?"

I watched her face. See what? I wondered.

She turned to me. "Coxley was the lawyer who sold me the house. We met once, very briefly. I wondered about him then. There was something about him . . ." She shook her head. "Chief Minister of Justice! I fear for the kingdom."

I thought of Gregor, who would occupy the throne with the devil himself as his most powerful official. With any luck, Coxley would be dead and gone when that day came.

"Beryl," I said, taking her hands, "Coxley worked for my father. He had them killed. I'm sure of it. He as much as said so to me. He said that seeing me dead would complete his unfinished work. He was gloating over it!" I felt my eyes grow wet.

Beryl frowned and nodded.

"Why would he do that?" Peter asked.

"For their wealth," Beryl said. "Perhaps, even, for some petty offense they caused him. But surely, for their wealth. To him, they were stepping-stones. How else does an unknown lawyer become the king's Chief Minister of Justice in so short a time?"

My breath came in little gasps. "Aunt always loved to say how my parents died in debt, that they were frauds, living high. I never believed it. But when they died, all the money was gone." I hated for Peter to see me cry like this.

"Men like Coxley are ruthless," Beryl said. "They'll stop at nothing to achieve their ends." She rose, rubbing her hands together briskly. "He stationed a guard here before leaving," she said, "out in the hedgerow beyond the property. If your goat hadn't made me aware of him, Lucinda, we'd be in trouble right now. As it is, I've taken care of him."

I felt a chill run over me, and for a moment I remembered the story of Aunt's brother, John. "Taken *care* of him? What did you do?"

Beryl shook her head with a wry smile. "He's fine, Lucinda. He'll wake up tomorrow thinking he had a rough night with the lads at a pub, and wander home to his wife. Now, come along, you two, we can't stay here. I'm afraid Coxley'll be back, possibly this time with company. We have an important mission." She patted her pocket and smiled. "Now that I have this back, I'm not afraid of what may come to me, but I have to keep you safe, Lucinda, until we can think of what to do about Coxley."

I stood with an effort, my tired legs protesting. "Where are we going?"

"To Montescue's Goldsmithy."

Chapter 24

The hansom cab disgorged us outside the faded door to Uncle's—now, Aunt's—shop. Beryl paid the driver, handing him a folded slip of paper and some extra money, along with some whispered instructions.

"What was that about?" I asked her.

"A message," she said, her lips tight. "Never mind that."

I looked up at the MONTESCUE'S sign painted over the shop window. Even with Beryl there to support me, I dreaded going inside and facing Aunt again.

We entered, Peter brushing crumbs from the sticky buns Beryl had bought us off his coat. The shop was empty. No one had dusted it since I left, that was plain.

I was beginning to wonder if Aunt would appear at all, when I heard a shuffling footstep coming down the stairs. She rounded the doorpost and stopped still, staring at the three of us.

She looked terrible. All the color was drained from her face, except the red rimming her eyes, and the red splotches on her nose and cheeks that she always wore when she went looking for liquid comfort.

"What do you want?" she said, her voice thick and hoarse. "What're you two doing together, and what gives you the nerve to come around here?"

I looked to Beryl to speak, and saw that she, herself, was trembling with fear.

"Haven't you caused me enough trouble?" Aunt went on, pointing a shaky finger at me. "Constables coming in here, not half an hour ago, and the Lord Minister of Justice himself, asking me if I've seen you anywhere." She gestured toward the window. "Tied his big black horse up right outside this door. Asked if I know where the stone you stole last night was. What'd you do, steal it again?"

They were still searching for me! The clop of a horseshoe on the street outside made me jump, but it was only a mule and a coal cart.

"Get that witch out of my shop," Aunt said.

"This is Beryl," I said to Aunt, my own voice faltering. "She's not a witch. She has something to say to you that you need to hear."

"Is this about the big jewel?" Aunt said, her consonants slurring.

"No," Beryl said softly. "It's about John."

Aunt faltered and caught herself on the countertop.

Beryl hurried forward to assist her. Aunt glared at her, and Beryl shrank back.

"Who *are* you?" Aunt said, her voice full of loathing.

Beryl knelt down on the floor and unwrapped the packages she'd brought. She placed them on the countertop, first the handsome youth, John, and then his sister, little curly-haired Hortensia, who was Aunt herself.

Aunt clapped a hand over her mouth. Her breathing became so shaky, I feared for her heart. Her eyes rained tears that dripped through her fingers onto her bosom.

"May I speak to you privately, Mrs. Montescue?" Beryl said. "There are things I need to say to you."

Aunt stood frozen, weeping and staring at the pictures. She nodded, once, and turned on her heel and walked out of the shop and up the stairs leading to the parlor. Beryl looked to me for guidance. I gestured for her to follow Aunt. Beryl went, looking as though she wished I would come. But my presence wouldn't help Aunt any. I stayed behind to make sure Peter didn't steal anything from the shop and to watch for returning constables.

Peter quickly grew tired of me policing him and sank down to snooze in a chair by the door. I paced the floor, straining my ears for some hint of what was happening upstairs and jumping at every shadow that passed by the windows. The sun sank behind the rooftops, and, I reminded myself, it was no longer my duty nor my privilege to light the lamps.

At last Beryl slipped through the door to the hall. She walked as if in a daze, but when she saw us she quickened her step.

"Let's hurry home," she said. "Coxley's still roaming the streets searching, and that gives us just enough time to do what we need to do."

◆　◆　◆

We rode home in silence, Beryl and I deep in thought, and Peter deep in sleep. When we reached the house, Beryl made us wait outside while she searched for evidence of another intruder, but at length she pronounced it safe for us to come inside. We both collapsed on couches in the parlor, where Beryl lit a fire.

"Take a little nap," Beryl said. "A pinch of rest would do you good."

I yawned. "I don't need a little naaaaaaaaaahp . . ."

And the next thing I knew, Beryl was waking me up, my head so woolly she could have persuaded me it was Christmas.

"How long did I sleep?"

"Half an hour," she said with a mysterious little smile. She handed me two thick slices of buttered bread.

I devoured a slice. A thought occurred to me as I chewed. "Did you make me sleep?"

She winked at me. "Your bath is heating by the fire-place in your room, and your clothes are pressed and ready. You need to wake up, too, Peter," she called loudly into his ear. "Your bath is heating in the kitchen. You both have an important engagement tonight."

Peter? Bath? Clothes? What was going on? I bit into the other slice of bread. I hadn't realized how famished I was.

"What engagement?" I pressed, still groggy with sleep. "I don't have any engagement."

"The carriage will be here in less than an hour. Here, unlace your boots."

Peter sat up, his hair sticking out in every direction. "What carriage?"

"One I've hired," Beryl said. "What a busy afternoon I've had. But everything is nearly ready. Get up! There's no time."

I peeled the blankets off me. "Beryl, what engagement are you talking about?"

She placed both fists on her hips. "The prince's ball, of course! What else?"

The ball!

To see Gregor one more time, if only from a distance. A far, safe distance . . .

What was I thinking? After he'd asked me not to? For shame!

I sank back down on the couch. "You're raving. I'm not going."

"Clothes, you say?" Peter asked. "You got some fancy togs for me?"

"I surely do." Beryl grinned. "You'll look like a young lord."

"Good enough," Peter said, rising to his feet. "I'm up for a lark."

"Sit down!" I yelled. "Peter, tell her why we're not going. Tell her what Gregor said."

He shrugged. "Some mumbledy-tosh about duty, and the princess. Who cares? There'll be hundreds of people at the ball. Wear a mask if you want. Let's go for the scenery."

Beryl snapped her fingers at Peter. "A mask. You are a genius."

He bowed his head modestly. "It's a known fact."

I threw up my hands. "You're a pair of fools. Why don't you go to the ball, Beryl, since you're so keen to. You can wear the mask."

Beryl shook her head. "I have an engagement of my own. You, Miss Lucinda, will be the envy of the ball to-night. Come and see what I have for you."

"No." I folded my arms across my chest. "Coxley is sure to be there. No ball is worth dying for."

"I can guarantee that Coxley won't be at the ball tonight," Beryl said.

"How do you know?"

"I know."

I scowled at her. I wasn't convinced.

She relented. "I have issued him an invitation," she said,

"which I am sure he will not refuse. Your path to the ball lies clear tonight."

"An *invitation*? Beryl, what are you trying to do?"

Beryl's jaw was set. "That is my business." She relaxed. "Lucinda, he can't hurt me."

That was true. I felt a little blossom of hope poke up inside me. Then I poked it back down.

"I can't face Gregor," I told her. "Not after all that's happened. He told me not to come."

Beryl dropped down onto the couch beside me and took both my hands in hers. "Lucinda, please," she said, her eyes imploring. "Trust me."

I could think of nothing to say.

"I would never wish you harm," Beryl said.

"But you have a way of exposing me to it, all the same," I said.

She had the grace to acknowledge this. "Not tonight. Tonight is different. I can feel it. You must go to the ball."

Peter, who'd been leaning against the fireplace, said, "You females! You know you're dying to go see Prince Gregor pledge his undying love to Princess Beatrix. You'd eat your heart out to miss that."

"Turn him into a toad, will you?" I asked Beryl, indicating Peter. "I'm sure you could."

"If I do, will you go to the ball?"

"Hey!" Peter yelped.

I rose with all the dignity I could muster. "You're wrong about females, Toad. But I suppose Gregor's ball would be the last place Coxley would look for me tonight. So I may as well spend my last night at a ball before I flee the country. I have nothing more to lose."

Beryl clapped her hands. "Come. Time's wasting. Peter, your bath and your things are in the kitchen. You're on your own. I'll be upstairs getting Lucinda ready."

◆ ◆ ◆

Half an hour later I sat at my mother's dressing table, drowsy from my bath, wrapped in a cotton robe. Beryl had toweled my wet hair until my scalp ached, but still it was damp. She fussed and fretted, then finally muttered some words I couldn't understand under her breath. A hot wind blew through the room, lifting my hair into a dark brown cloud. It passed just as suddenly, leaving me completely dry.

I asked no questions.

"That's better," Beryl said, patting the stone in her pocket. "It's good to have it back." She set to work combing out the tangles in my hair. She brushed it in long, smooth strokes using Mama's silver brush. She'd polished its tarnished handle since yesterday, I noticed.

When the brushing was done, she set to work coiling and braiding my hair. Her fingers flew, snatching little sections and knotting them around her knuckles, twisting in lengths of beaded ribbon. I frowned at my reflection in the mirror.

"I look ridiculous," I said.

"Patience," she said through a mouth full of hairpins.

When at last the coiffure was finished, I eyed myself skeptically. Yes, it was well done, but it didn't feel like me at all.

"This way," she said, leading me to the dressing room. She thrust the candlestick toward me. "Take off everything, and put these on"—she handed me silk underthings and a petticoat—"and these"—a pair of fine ivory stockings—"and this." She pointed to a cream bodice draped over a fabric bust. "I'll help you with the rest. Don't muss your hair, whatever you do." She stepped out and pulled the door shut behind her.

There was nothing to do but comply. I dropped my robe and picked up the flimsy underthings. They were so slippery-soft and tickly against my skin that I nearly giggled. I pulled on the stockings, unrolling them up my legs, and fastened the garters. I'd never worn anything half so fine, not even the day I'd gone to the Winter Festival.

I pulled the cream bodice over me, but I couldn't reach the buttons in the back.

"Beryl?"

She opened the door, fastened my buttons, and assaulted me with a glass perfume wand, stroking scent against my neck and arms. Then she held at my feet what looked like a tube of crumpled red satin. "Step in," she commanded. I did so, and she pulled up a crimson gown and helped me stuff my arms into the sleeves. She pulled the corset tight in the back until I gasped.

"I'm afraid your mother was a smaller woman than you," Beryl observed.

The thought puzzled me. She was always bigger than me in memory. Had I really grown larger? How could I ever be larger than Mama?

"Now these," she said, holding a pair of beaded pearl-colored slippers. I slipped my feet into them, and miraculously, they fit.

"Mama must have had big feet, anyway," I said.

"Mmm," Beryl said enigmatically.

"Did you magic the slippers?" I demanded.

"Ask me no questions," she said, "and I'll tell you no lies." She spun me around by the shoulders and draped a necklace over me, fastening it in the back. She spun me once more and clipped a pair of earrings onto my earlobes. They pinched.

Then she paraded me back to the dressing table and sat me down before it.

"There now," she said.

I broke out in goose pimples. Looking back at me from Mama's mirror was someone else. Like a ghost of Mama, but different.

Like a princess.

The gown circled low over my shoulders, leaving my neck bare. Through the magic of dressmaking, or perhaps some extra magic, I suddenly had a figure. The gold and onyx necklace she'd put on me gleamed dark against my pale skin. Lace trim from the underbodice peeked out underneath my red gown, which fit snugly until it tapered to a point at my waist. From there it billowed into voluminous skirts that swished with each movement.

I stood up, tripping on the heel of my slipper and clutching at the necklace.

"I can't do it, Beryl, that's not me. I'll make a fool of myself. I can't carry it off." I tugged at the necklace, but it wouldn't yield. "Please don't make me. I'm bound to fail."

Beryl placed both hands on my shoulders. I felt calm flow into me through her. She gave me a long look through the mirror.

"Don't be frightened by your beauty, Lucinda," she said. "You haven't, until now, known you had it, and so you're uncorrupted by it. You can never take any credit for it, or make it your aim." She smiled. "But it would be as much an act of deceit to deny your beauty or tell yourself that what you see is not you. Beauty hovers around you wherever you go, which is why these two poor young men chase after you when you're covered in dirt and dressed in rags. Not beauty of the face or form. Something eternal. This beauty that comes from dresses and jewels"—she paused to tuck a curl of my hair back into place—"is somewhat of an illusion. But even illusion has its place. And that's what parties and dancing are for."

She bent and kissed my forehead. "Go be beautiful tonight, my dear," she said. "Your mother and father would burst with pride if they could see you right now."

My eyes filled with tears.

"Heavens, don't do that," Beryl said, thrusting a handkerchief at me. "Nothing like crying to break the illusion."

I wiped my eyes and laughed.

One word she'd used stuck with me. Now, tonight, with Mama almost looking back at me through the mirror, I dared to ask the question it raised.

"Beryl," I said, "you're . . . eternal yourself. The priests in this world teach that life, even for mortals, goes on after death, in some other place. Is that true? Do you know? Is your world our heaven?"

She pulled a stem from a vase of flowers on the dressing table and trimmed its end, her face thoughtful. It was her favorite flower, the love-lies-bleeding. The name she'd given herself, meaning deathless—*amaranth*.

"My world is not your heaven," she said, stroking the blossoms. "That I know. But sometimes I find, in the writings of your poets, words that make me feel as though they've been to my home. Which is why I don't read poetry much anymore. It hurts too much." She tucked the stem behind my ear. "This, I think—for all the frailties and cruelties and stupidities of your kind, you're still too much like us not to be eternal, at least in some way. You're all too valuable to be disposable."

I frowned, skeptical. "Even Coxley?"

She turned, a look of surprise on her face. "Oh, my dear, haven't you figured it out? I thought you must have." She rubbed a hand across her forehead. "Coxley isn't from your world. He's from mine."

Chapter 25

Carriage!" Peter bellowed up the stairs.

I turned to face her. "If he can't ever die, then he'll never stop chasing me." I felt my breath catch in my throat. "I'll never be rid of him. And I won't be able to stay here with you. I'll have to flee."

Beryl cocked her head to one side. "With me?"

I looked at her. "Yes, with you. Don't you want to stay?"

She brushed a strand of hair off my forehead. "Do you want me to?"

"Of course I do!" I leaned forward and embraced her. "That is, I would if I could. What good is a big house without some company?"

Beryl took her time disentangling herself from my hug. She draped a fur-lined stole over my shoulders. "It will be cold in the carriage."

I held her face with both hands. "I don't want to lose you, Beryl."

She gently removed my hands from her face and pressed them between her own.

"Nor I you," she said. "Remember that. Don't be afraid, and don't lose hope. I may be able to do something about Coxley. Hush now." She dabbed at me once more with a kerchief.

"Carriage!" Peter called once more.

"Coming," Beryl replied. She opened a drawer on Mama's dressing table and pulled something out. "For your hands," she said, offering me gloves, and then, "for your face." She held up a black feathered mask attached to a slim wand.

I tested its appearance in the mirror. It gave the stranger in the red gown an exotic, mysterious look.

"Was this Mama's?" I asked, incredulous.

"It certainly isn't mine," Beryl said.

"I'm going without you," Peter called, his voice now coming from the hallway.

"Now," Beryl whispered, "go give that prince of yours something to think about."

My jaw dropped. Beryl winked, and beckoned me out the door.

I followed her into the candlelit hallway. There stood Peter, his hands on his waist, posing for us in his finery.

And not without cause. I wouldn't have recognized him. His once-mangy hair was washed and shining, tied in back with a black ribbon. He wore a resplendent amber coat with broad cuffs and lapels, all magnificently embroidered with black and purple twist, and a snow white lace cravat at his throat, over black hose and gleaming shoes with silver buckles.

I was trying to think up a suitable compliment that wouldn't inflate his vanity too much when I noticed his expression.

He was gaping at me. Specifically, at my dress. His eyes bulged like a fresh-caught fish's.

I pulled my wrap tight around me and brushed past him down the stairs.

"Weren't you the one in a great hurry, Peter?" I called over my shoulder.

I reached the door and looked back. Peter descended in a daze, nudged along by Beryl.

"If you dawdle any more you'll miss the reception line," she said, nearly pushing Peter headlong down the stairs. "Then you won't be presented to the king and queen."

"Reason enough for me," I said, heading back up the stairs. "I'm not sure this dress fits, let's go find another one. . . ."

Beryl blocked my path with a smile on her face that didn't hide her resolve.

"The dress fits," Beryl said. "Doesn't it, Peter?"

"Um-hmm," Peter said, his face flushing.

I glared at him.

"W-well enough, I mean to say," he stammered.

I groaned. Reception line? Presented to the king and queen? "Beryl, must I go?"

She nodded. "You must. If only to show the palace how you look tonight."

"That's a ridiculous reason and you know it," I said. "Must I go with *him*? He's sure to steal my earrings." I bit my lip to hide a grin.

Beryl fixed Peter with a stern look. "Peter, do you promise to steal nothing this night?"

Peter's forehead creased with thought. "I promise not to steal . . . from Lucinda."

"Fair enough," Beryl pronounced. She reached for the doorknob and shooed us both out.

The cold sent a shock through me. It made the night sky feel huge and barren. Even so, far beyond my reach, millions of stars blazed in the heavens. The moon, just past full, hung low and fat over the house.

"Don't come back until midnight at least," Beryl called.

Peter sprinted down the walk toward the carriage and held the door for me, shivering.

At the sight of the carriage, I drew in my breath. It was pale and glistening, small and graceful, like my pearl dancing shoes. A team of four white mares with braided manes stamped their hooves, eager to get moving. The driver, swaddled toe to chin in wraps, waved to us.

I allowed Peter to help me in. He fell into the seat beside me as the horses took off. With four of them pulling such a light vehicle, we fairly flew over bumps in the road.

"Where'd she find this carriage?" Peter said. "It beats Prince Gregor's by half."

"Does it?" I remembered my earlier ride. "You seem to be a connoisseur of carriages."

"Plan to have some of my own, someday," Peter said.

This caught my attention. "With all your thieving and profiteering, you ought to live like a lord. What d'you do with all your money?"

"Save it," he said.

"Such discipline! What for?"

"Just what you said. I ought to live like a lord. And I aim to."

That Peter had a driving ambition fascinated me. There was a purpose to his depravity! "So, you'll buy yourself a chateau somewhere and live a life of retirement and ease?"

"I don't know about 'retirement,'" he said. "I'll keep busy enough. But I don't just want to live *like* a lord. I want to be one."

I turned to face him, but of course, he was only a hole in the darkness. "You *what?*"

He hesitated. "I want to be one. Be a lord." He sounded defensive.

I tried not to laugh. "But how can you?"

"Buy a peerage."

He made it sound like the most mundane thing imaginable, like buying a spool of thread or a pennyworth of salt. Buy a peerage. Buy a named title and the lands and estates that went with it. Why shouldn't a street thief do that?

"But surely," I said, "a peerage itself would be a vast amount. And then you'd need capital to live on, to invest, to build, to operate. Why not keep the money and simply live as a rich man in a fine house somewhere?"

The fervor in Peter's answer surprised me. "Because my whole life I've looked around me and thought, 'What puts you here at the bottom, Peter, and those high-and-mighties up top?' Are they cleverer than me? Not likely. Harder working? Not on your silver buttons."

I fingered the front of my gown. No silver buttons.

" 'Make way for Lord Fleur-de-lis,' " he mimicked. " 'Bow to Lady Beauregard.' 'Clear the area; Count Rymington and his party are arriving.' What makes them better than me?"

Possibly, the fact that they aren't criminals, I thought of pointing out, but he was so overcome by the violence of this passion that I stayed still.

"Make no mistake, though," he said, "I've sold to most of the men, and bought from all the ladies, too, when their finances get pinched. They're not all so grand as they like to make out. And someday I'll be Sir Peter Such-and-such, their financier, who makes discreet loans at high interest, and they'll come groveling to *me*. And we'll see who's bowing then."

I'd never seen him like this before. I listened to the creak of the carriage wood filling the night and thought of all I'd learned about Peter in just a few short days. He was a rascal, a liar, and a bare-faced cheat, and yet he seemed as inevitable as a force of nature.

"Well, Peter," I said, "it's a bold ambition, but you'll do it, if you're not murdered first."

"Oh, I won't be," he said. "I'm much too careful for that."

The rattle of wheels on cobblestones showed we'd reached the city. Lights from homes and shops reflected inside the carriage, and I took a better look at Peter. In the dim light he looked pale and moody, somber as a judge.

A generous impulse overtook me. "You look fine, Peter. The clothes suit you well."

He looked at me, his face unreadable. "You're toying with me. Like at the festival."

That he should think such a thing! "Indeed, I'm not. But if you won't have my compliments, never mind."

The palace came into view. Every window blazed with light. I felt suddenly clammy with sweat, even in the cold.

The mask. I held it up to my face. Could I, perhaps, wear it all evening and remain hidden from Gregor as a silent observer? I tried it on again, for practice.

"You look quite nice, too," Peter said, startling me.

"Now that I have the mask on? Thank you kindly."

"No," he said. "With or without the mask. More so without it, I'd say."

I made a show of wiggling a finger in my ear. "Is this Peter talking? Is there another girl in the carriage?"

He looked out the window. We couldn't see the palace anymore; we were approaching it head-on, and nearly there.

"Come, come," I said. "You may be a lord someday, but you aren't one yet. No need for the courtly manners, and certainly not the moody temper. If you're to be my escort tonight, I insist you be a cheery one. You can even insult me if you like. It always makes you feel better."

The carriage pulled up at the drive and stopped. Up the sweeping granite staircase I saw the broad doors thrown open to admit other new arrivals. It might have been noonday inside, so many lamps were lit.

And somewhere in this glittering chaos was Gregor. I reminded myself to breathe. And breathe again.

I stood on the curb with no notion of how I'd exited the carriage. The driver chirruped to the team and moved off toward the stables.

Don't leave me here, pretty horses.

We both stood, looking up, speechless. A line of footmen in powdered wigs and matching gray jackets stood at attention, clearly wondering why we didn't approach.

"You've been here often, haven't you?" I whispered to Peter.

"Never through this door," he said.

He held out his arm, and I took it. I was bound to

stumble in these infernal slippers. I had no practice moving about in such foolishness.

I used my free hand to hold my mask in place, and concentrated on each step to avoid looking at the door.

A tall, dour-faced man stood by the doorkeeper. He'd probably been greeting palace guests since the Flood. He inspected us up and down as if committing us to memory, and asked, in a voice as deep as the grave, "Your names?"

Oh dear. I hadn't thought about that.

"Dorian Carlucci," Peter said, and elbowed me under the cover of my wraps. The man frowned at Peter, looking down at him through his small spectacles.

Not my true name. Whom should I be tonight? Angelica? Gregor would recognize that.

What to say?

"Mask off, please, mademoiselle," the man said. I lowered the wand.

"Beryl White," I told Sir Serious. It was the first thing that came to mind. Peter gave me a sideways glance.

"Of?"

I held my head high. "Of the Palisades."

Sir Serious took a closer look at me, but nodded to the doorman, who pushed the vast door open.

Chapter 26

And we were in. I clapped the mask back over my face.

A bowing manservant relieved me of my wrap and whisked it away. Without it I felt exposed in my red gown. I'd never worn anything quite so tight. I didn't see anyone else wearing a mask, which made me nervous, but still I hid my face.

I couldn't see the floor for all the swishing skirts. The air was thick with dizzying perfumes, sizzling savory fragrances, and the bewildering scent of wine. It was hot and steamy, swirling with light and smoke from a thousand candles. Music came from somewhere, though I couldn't make out the tune exactly over the buzzing voices.

No sign of Gregor, thank heaven. Yet that didn't stop me from searching for him.

It felt terribly lonely to enter a room so full and know

that no one cared if I was there. But soon I wished I was merely anonymous. Staring eyes were everywhere.

A stout gentleman passed by, brushing into Peter. Peter's hand followed him, reaching for a leather case that jutted out of the man's pocket.

I yanked him back sharply. "Are you daft?"

Peter leaned over and whispered, through smiling teeth, "I could have a heyday in here in under five minutes."

Was there no limit to his nerve? "Don't you dare."

Peter sighed and patted my hand, which still rested on his forearm. "Do you realize what you're depriving me of?"

I pretended to straighten his lapel, but instead, yanked it tight till I had his full attention. "I won't be arrested again, Peter. Not tonight. Understand?"

He rolled his eyes.

I leaned closer to whisper even softer. "Why are they staring at us?"

"Maybe it's your mask," he said. "This isn't a costume party."

"I know," I said miserably. "But I don't dare take it off. Can we leave now?"

Faces half-concealed by pince-nez and fans turned our way and whispered to one another. Heads towering tall with powdered hair wagged in our direction. Their notice seemed to spread like ripples in a pond.

Young women's eyes sized Peter up then turned to me. They lingered on my mask. I knew it was out of place, yet the more people stared at it the more I dreaded ever removing it.

"All the ladies envy me, Peter," I said. "You shall have your pick of dancing partners."

Peter thrust his chest out even farther, if such a thing were possible. "I am devastating, aren't I? Togs like these suit me. In two years' time, I'll own a dozen sets."

Another servant appeared with a tray of small meat pastries. At the sight of them my stomach growled, but I hesitated. Peter, whose ease I envied, took two and offered me one.

The serving man nodded toward a tall double doorway. "The line begins over there."

Poking out from the doorway was the end of a long queue of couples that disappeared from view inside the next room. With a sinking heart, I stepped closer until I saw. We weren't even in the ball proper. This was merely a foyer.

Peter steered me toward the end of the line. From there I could see into the grand ballroom. It dwarfed the room we'd first entered. Here the music was louder, the lights brighter, and the assembly even more vast and colorful. The orchestra played in a balcony, and dancers made good use of the floor. On a dais at the head of the room, festooned with flowers and ribbons, stood four tall thrones. King Hubert and Queen Rosamond, both round and beaming, sat in two, and another regal couple in the others. The king and queen of Hilarion. It had to be. For standing between the two pairs of thrones were Gregor and Princess Beatrix, arm-in-arm.

He'd never looked better.

Nor, I imagined, had she.

The line moved closer and I got a better view of the princess. She was swathed from shoulder to toe in rose silk—no match for the roses in her cheeks. The pearls at her throat were so large they reminded me of Beryl's stone. Her flaxen hair was done up in curls that tumbled gracefully down over her shoulders, with a tall, delicate lace cap nestled on top. She held a dainty hand out for each guest to kiss, and gave all her sweetest smile and curtsy.

From this closer distance I could see even more clearly how exquisitely pleasing her features were. In beauty and manners she was everything a princess ought to be. She would make an exemplary queen someday.

And she was standing much closer to Gregor than I fancied.

Gregor stood erect in his royal red coat and tails, trimmed with medals and ribbons, an ornamental sword belt draped over one shoulder. He greeted each guest, acknowledging them affably. Beside him Princess Beatrix reached only to his chest in height, but he smiled down upon her, obviously pleased by her every word.

He's happy now, I realized. He's sorted himself out,

and he's got what he always wanted. He loves her, or, at least, is starting to.

Who wouldn't?

Besides me, I mean.

How could I come here, against his express wishes, and complicate his happiness? What kind of fiend was I?

How did I let Beryl talk me into this?

It wasn't Beryl's fault. I'd come because I wanted to. What madness makes us seek to see our own worst torment?

Worse still, I'd come with a tiny hope, born of seeing myself in the mirror, and hearing all of Peter's flattery. I'd imagined that, maybe, once Gregor saw me, if he did, he'd . . .

I couldn't bear now to complete the thought.

We drew closer. The line ahead of us dwindled alarmingly as each group of worshippers paid their respects and were absorbed into the dance or the refreshment tables or the rooms where cigars fumed and cards and billiards were played.

I made up my mind. I would do nothing to disturb Gregor's peace or his plans. If I truly cared for him—if I loved him—there was no other honorable choice than to hide behind my mask. If my mask would hide me.

And did I love him?

The flickering candles in hundreds of lamps reminded me of the candles in his chapel.

Oh, my heart. I did.

If only he weren't a prince. If only he was a poor peasant somewhere, I could be a poor peasant beside him. All I'd ask for was his smile, and endless dancing lessons. But he *was* a prince, and not just in name. He deserved a greater heart than mine.

"Peter," I whispered. "This is important. Do I look like myself?"

"No," he said. "You look like her." He pointed to a stout older woman holding court in an alcove with a circle of weary listeners and a plate of hot dainties.

"Be serious," I said. "Do I look like myself?"

"This is an odd time to fish for compliments."

I groaned. "I'm not, you idiot. I mean, am I recognizable? Will Gregor know me?"

Peter gave me an appraising look. "If he doesn't, he'll want to."

I felt my cheeks grow warm.

"Don't be silly," I said. "Not while he's got such a vision there beside him."

Peter looked up at the dais. He said nothing. We took another step forward.

I'd get no useful information from him. To soothe my nerves I changed the subject.

"What do you think of the princess?"

He looked again at her. "She is very beautiful." He seemed to choose his words carefully.

"Obviously," I said. "But what do you think of her?"

We stepped forward again. I could hear their voices now, talking with guests. Princess Beatrix's voice rose like a melody over the hum of voices in the room.

Peter looked at me. He seemed unusually serious. "What I think of her is unimportant."

An odd answer. But I had no chance to puzzle out its meaning, for now there was only one couple before us, kissing the king and queen of Hilarion on their outstretched hands.

I tried to swallow but couldn't. I didn't know what to do with my hands, and I felt certain I'd trip and fall onto the dais.

Their Graces of Hilarion finished with that couple and turned their tired eyes our way.

Peter hoisted me forward. Odd that I should be schooled in social graces by a street thief.

"Dorian Carlucci," Peter said, bowing low before their thrones.

"Beryl White," I said. I curtsyed so low my knees nearly buckled.

Gregor was so close I could smell his cologne. I kept my masked eyes on the floor.

"Charmed to meet you both," said the king.

"Enchanted," added the queen.

"Welcome to Saint Sebastien," Peter added for good measure.

We kissed their hands and moved down the line, to stand before the future king and queen of Laurenz, who stood glowing with mutual adoration.

Out of the corner of my eye, I saw Peter struggle to hide a smirk.

What a fool I'd been! Even if I'd come wrapped in a Bedouin's robes, Gregor would recognize Peter. From there my identity would easily follow.

"Dorian Carlucci," Peter said.

"No, you're not," Gregor said, grinning broadly.

"Beryl White," I whispered, feeling faint.

"Darling, do you know these people?" the princess purred.

"This one owes me money," Gregor said. "How did you get in here, you rogue? You must have hoodwinked Bartholemew." He sounded amused, which was some relief. Not much, but some.

"It wouldn't do to miss the party," Peter said. He made a flamboyant bow. "Now that you've been sold off the market, I had to give the brokenhearted young ladies of Laurenz some consolation."

"In that case you ought not to have brought such a charming companion," Gregor said, tapping his chin. "Why would she hide behind that mask, I wonder?"

Princess Beatrix stood taller and inched closer to him.

"Pox," I whispered. The princess let out a little mew of fright.

"Scars," I added hastily. "Years ago."

"Pity," Gregor said, raising an eyebrow.

A note in his voice alarmed me. Did he suspect? Or was I imagining?

"My dear," the princess said to me, "what is that charming weed you have behind your ear? Darling," she crooned, addressing Gregor, "you haven't introduced me properly to this dashing young friend of yours." She fluttered her fan and turned the full force of her smile upon Peter.

She's paying you back for complimenting me, Gregor. Tit-for-tat.

"Call him any name you like," Gregor said. "As long as you call him with gold in your pocket, he'll answer." He spoke to the princess, but his eyes were on me.

"What a thing to say!" the princess said. "I can see, Miss White, that I shall need to teach your prince some manners."

I bowed my head. I preferred that my prince's manners remain untouched by hers.

"Are Their Highnesses acquainted with your friends?" the princess continued. She took hold of Peter's hand, leading him over to where King Hubert and Queen Rosamond sat on their cushioned thrones.

"Mother, Father," Gregor said, "these are some friends of mine. May I present," he gave me a sideways glance that made my insides squirm, "Mister Dorian Carlucci, and his fair companion, Miss Beryl White?"

Peter bowed and I curtsyed.

"Why do you wear that mask, my dear?" Queen Rosamond demanded. "Masks haven't been in fashion these ten years or more."

I made an apologetic bow.

"Well, take it off. Let's see your face!" She smiled but expected obedience.

Gregor's face registered alarm. I could barely move.

"Mother, I believe Miss White has her reasons—"

"Fiddle-faddle," the queen interrupted.

"*Dear*," King Hubert said severely, putting an end to the discussion. Bless his bald head. I could almost forgive him for sending me to the gallows only the day before.

"Tell me, young man," the king said, addressing Peter, "who are your people?"

"Merchants," Peter said quickly, "from northern Italy. Trading in diamonds and exotic gems from Africa and the Orient."

Peter could lie more naturally than most people spoke truth. More power to him, so long as he kept the others' attention off me.

"How fascinating!" Queen Rosamond sat up straighter in her chair.

"You don't look Italian," King Hubert said, frowning.

Queen Rosamond swatted at him. "'Course he does. He said Northern Italy! Now tell me, young man," she said, gesturing him nearer, "since you're an expert, what do you think of our delightful Beatrix's pearls there? Have you ever in your life seen such a set?"

Peter turned and studied her. She blushed obligingly.

"May I?" Peter said, reaching out a hand. Beatrix leaned over to give Peter the best view of her pearls. Among other things.

Queen Rosamond's eyes were riveted upon Peter.

He rolled a pearl between his thumb and forefinger, then turned back to the queen. "She wears them well, Your Highness," Peter said, "but they're fake."

Princess Beatrix stood straight and squealed. "Never!"

"I say!" King Hubert cried.

Queen Rosamond, her mouth agape, rose trembling from her throne. Apparently fake pearls were something she took deeply to heart. Had she given them as a gift? This royal family had unfortunate luck in its jewel purchases.

She leveled a quavering arm in Peter's direction. "Young man," she said, her voice sounding choked, "you are not who you say you are."

Oh no.

Peter stepped back, his eyes darting about for an exit. He had guilt written all over him.

What had he said, about sleeping at the king's summer house? Curse you, Peter! What'd you do, steal the queen's crown last June?

"Hubert," the queen said urgently. "His face. Do you see it? Do you remember?"

The king squinted at Peter from under his bushy eyebrows. "It can't be!" He peered closer. "Can it?"

Peter and I exchanged a look of alarm.

"What's going on here?" Gregor demanded.

Peter took that as his chance to turn heel and dash away through the crowd. He crashed into my arm and shattered the fragile spindle that held my mask. It fell to the ground, along with my amaranth blossom.

Gregor's eyes met mine. His held no surprise. Only pain.

For a moment time stopped. Then the spell was severed.

Queen Rosamond swooned, slumping heavily back into her throne. Princess Beatrix shrieked. King Hubert shot out of his chair to attend the queen, shouting over his shoulder, "Stop him! Guards! Don't let him get away!"

A whistle blew. Constables and palace guards began streaming in through the doors.

Peter cut a streak of chaos through the dancers.

"Salts," Gregor called to a servant. "And wine. Quickly. The queen is ill."

I started to sidle away.

"She doesn't have scars on her face," Princess Beatrix said indignantly, pointing at me.

"Who the devil cares about *her* face?" King Hubert roared, fanning the air under Queen Rosamund's nose. "My wife's fainted! Call a doctor!"

It was the last I heard from the royals on the dais.

Guards flew one way and servants another, and amid the commotion, I turned around, looking for a way to disappear into the crowd. My scanning eyes caught sight of a tall figure in uniform striding in behind an advance guard of police sergeants.

Coxley. Heading straight for the royal dais.

I hitched up my skirts and ran.

Chapter 27

I pushed and elbowed my way through the crowd of sweaty, powdered ladies and tobacco-smelling men, all together agog at what had happened to the queen. Shouting voices rose behind me, and for one panicked moment I relived my arrest at the Winter Festival. But the voices were saying to stop *him*, not her, so no one paid me much heed as I made for the doors.

Had Coxley seen me?

Peter was the focus of attention, and I was glad of it. Knowing him he'd find a way out. I couldn't afford to get caught up in his trouble. Not with Coxley in the room.

But I wasn't altogether sure whether I was running from Coxley or from Gregor's eyes.

I slipped out through a side door. The foyer was nearly empty. People must have poured into the ballroom to see what was happening. I abandoned my fur wrap and shot out the door into the cold night.

My flimsy slippers threatened to fall off with each step down the stairs. Once one did, and I considered leaving it there, but one footfall in my stocking feet on the cold granite changed my mind. I shoved my foot back into the shoe and hurried on. At the bottom I ran through the dark along the curving drive until I smelled, then saw, the stables. Drivers and horsemen lounged in the doorway, smoking pipes. At the sound of my feet on the gravel, they straightened up.

"My carriage," I called. "I need to get home." My driver detached himself from the bunch and hurried back into the stables while I gathered my breath.

I felt self-conscious, alone with so many men. No less did they. I strained my ears for sounds of pursuit, for the galloping crunch of black hooves on stones.

"Do any of you know what time it is?" I asked.

One driver consulted a watch on a chain. "It lacks a quarter until ten."

Nowhere near midnight. But it couldn't be helped. Whatever purpose she'd had in sending me to the ball was foiled now by Peter, and Queen Rosamond's hysterical reaction to him. What could all that have meant?

The white horses appeared, hitched to the fairy carriage. "Where's your young man, miss?" the driver asked.

"We're not waiting for him," I said.

An anxious look crossed his face. "I'm charged to bring you both here and back."

I understood. "He's met up with some old friends. He's staying longer. They'll see him home." At this rate I'd soon be as good a liar as Peter.

The driver held the door for me, and I climbed in. The horses took off. Carriage wheels squeaked. The streets were empty at this hour, with half the city at the palace and the other half huddled in bed, so we fairly flew along.

I leaned back against the upholstery and closed my eyes. Gregor's grave and troubled face watched me all the way home.

In no time we were there. I thanked the driver, wishing I had a coin to give him. Before he drove away, I called out to him.

"Driver! Did you see or hear any sign of someone following us?"

He shook his head. His honest face suggested no deception.

I thanked him again, and hurried toward the door.

Something made me stop. I looked up at the house, which sat like a crouching giant on top of its rise of ground, a waning moon shining down on its towers and gables. The tall windows over the terrace—that had been the ballroom. On a night like tonight, if it weren't for Coxley's treachery all those years ago, those windows would gleam with candlelight reflecting off brass instruments, and swirling dancers, platters of meats, and vats of flaming punch.

All the windows, all the rooms, the places my parents slept and ate and cared for me. There they were. I had earned them back, and for what? I would never enjoy the house now. It felt like a cage, a trap. If I went into that box, Coxley might imprison me in it.

The thought of all I'd lost in these last days overwhelmed me.

Soon I would look for Beryl, but first I wanted a moment alone.

I turned from the house toward the gardens. Small gardens surrounded the house and dotted the lawns, but the real garden, my mother's favorite, stood some distance from the house, on a rise of ground, surrounded by trees. Too far away for Coxley to see me if he came looking, but open enough that I could watch for him and hide if he came.

Frozen grass snapped under my feet. My path was striped by the long shadows of trees. Night creatures scattered at my approach.

The garden sat like a Greek temple overlooking the house, with the moon as its chandelier. A yew hedge surrounded the hilltop. At the apex was a fountain with rows of plantings and walkways radiating outward. Marble columns reached to the heavens, and a statue of milk white lovers in the fountain sat entwined in an eternal embrace. My eyes lingered on Cupid's ardent form. Begone, thoughts of Gregor! I looked away.

Beryl's occasional helpers must have done some tending here. Even the withered stalks of summer's flowers and the thorny stems of last year's roses stood in frost-covered dignity. This had once been the masterpiece of the gardens, back when there was a staff to tend it. Mama used to spend hours here in the summertime, picking flowers and painting watercolors. My heart ached, thinking that this spring I would have dug and planted here myself.

"You still can," Beryl's voice said.

I jumped and turned around. There she was, sitting on a garden bench.

"Forgive me." She smiled. "I heard the carriage, and when you didn't come into the house, I came looking for you. So I snuck up on you *and* eavesdropped. Two unforgivable sins."

"That's all right." I sat beside her on the bench. "How'd you know what I was thinking?"

Beryl tapped the stone that hung at her breastbone. I saw that she'd woven herself a little pouch to carry it around her neck.

Instinctively, I reached out and touched the stone. One brush with my finger warmed my whole body. The gem glowed white, illuminating Beryl's face.

"Does the stone tell you what everyone is thinking?"

She shook her head. "No. Well, yes, in a way. You could say that with it, I'm more perceptive of the feelings of those around me. But it is only the people who are open to me, whose thoughts I can know well."

I rested my head upon her shoulder, looking around at Mama's garden. "I wish you could have known my parents."

Beryl leaned her head on mine. "I would like to have known them."

We sat.

Over the treetops the wind howled, but here in the garden the air was still. Warm, even. I suspected that had something to do with Beryl.

"How was the ball?"

I groaned.

"That bad?"

"Worse."

"What happened?"

"What *didn't* happen, you mean," I said. "Peter made the queen faint and the king yell for the guards to capture him. Gregor recognized me. He was *not* happy. Princess Beatrix gloated over me. And, just as I was trying to leave, Coxley showed up."

Beryl stiffened. "He did? Are you sure?"

I nodded. "Just before I left."

Beryl groaned and stretched her arms toward the sky.

"What's the matter?" I cried, alarmed for her.

She said nothing but shook her head miserably.

"What was the invitation you issued him?" I ventured.

Beryl was silent for a while, plucking at a hollow stalk of dried bamboo. "I lured him to the seashore," she said at last. "I told him I would be there, alone, with my stone."

I shook my head, disbelieving. "You challenged him to a *duel?* Coxley? Beryl, what were you thinking? He's a murderer!"

Beryl's face was grim. Immediately I regretted my choice of words.

"Lucinda, with my stone he couldn't hurt me," she said. "Not unless he took it from me. That's what he wants, don't you see? He's not after my stone for money, the way Peter was. Coxley had his own stone once. He knows what mine would give him. No secret would be safe from him, no plot against him could hope to succeed. With a stone he can deceive, and bind, and rule the entire kingdom of Laurenz. Perhaps the world."

Gregor. I saw him as he was tonight, standing in uniform in the throne room of the palace, with Coxley bursting through the door.

Beryl went on. "Without a stone, Coxley is a strong and evil man who'll never die. With a stone, he'd be worse than a devil. A . . ." She searched for a word. "A malevolent god."

I reached out again and touched Beryl's stone. "But he didn't get it from you."

She blew out her breath. "No, he didn't."

"Then, what happened?"

She stroked her stone. "I summoned him, thinking I could drive him out of the kingdom. Scare him away, if you will, like a fox driving another fox from its lair. For your sake. For my penance."

"Your penance?" I asked.

"My kind shouldn't be here with these stones, Lucinda. I brought this temptation here."

I tried to suppress my impatience. "So, what *happened?*"

She laughed faintly. "The women of Saint Sebastien would be aghast if they saw it. We fought. I ordered him to leave, with all the force my stone gives me, but he wouldn't go. So we fought. He was no match for me then, and he ran away. I chased him to the northernmost borders of Hilarion, then turned back here."

"But that's several weeks' journey!"

She smiled weakly. "Not for us. I thought I could show him there wasn't room for both of us in Laurenz. But I was wrong to hope it would work. He came back. And now I'll have to think of something else."

She was so disappointed, I wished I could comfort her. I had never expected her to rid me of Coxley.

"It's all right, Beryl," I said, looking out over my parents' garden. "There's nothing holding us here. We'll go away, far away from here, where Coxley can never find us."

Beryl didn't look convinced.

We sat and listened to the cold. Slowly, the tension and

fear I'd carried since I arrived at the ball began to slide off me. Gardens can do that, even at night, even in the wintertime. But Beryl sat morose and unaffected by the calm night.

"This is the longest night of the year," I said, thinking aloud. "The winter solstice. Christmas is in only a few days."

Beryl said nothing.

"At least you have your stone back in time for Christmas," I said. It was a feeble attempt to cheer her, and I knew it. But I hated to see her so low.

I reached for her hand.

"Thank you for everything, Beryl," I said. "You've given me so much."

She made a sound of protest. "I've given you nothing but sorrow!" she cried. Her eyes filled with tears. "It's you that has given to me."

I put my arms around her. "I had sorrows to begin with," I whispered in her ear. "You've given me things I would never have known. To dance with Gregor . . . that night will always be with me. And you let me come home. Being here in this place one more time is enough for me. I thought my memories of my parents had died long ago, but now I'll always carry them."

I left damp spots on her shoulder when I pulled myself away, a little embarrassed. When I looked back at Beryl, her violet eyes shone.

"Memories," she repeated eagerly. "That is one thing I can give you. May it ease some of the pain my errors have caused." She reached into the yarn pouch she'd fashioned and pulled out her stone. She placed it in my palm.

"Lucinda, show me this garden as you remember it."

Chapter 28

I took the stone reluctantly from her hand. It shone butter yellow and felt warm and moist in my hand, like a new apple.

"How?" I asked.

"Don't worry," she said. She wiped her eyes and laughed. The chimes of her voice rippled through the yew trees. "It will be easy. Light the stone, and enter it."

Enter it? I wanted to protest but something stopped me. Pleading weakness as an excuse no longer seemed like an option. The stone demanded more from me than that.

Light the stone. I held it before my face. Only moments ago it had lit while Beryl held it. Now it lay, cold and dark, in my palm.

Light it.

I squeezed it. *Light, please!*

The faintest gleam appeared. It gave me hope.

Like a sun, like a star, shine. Give us heat and light, in this longest night of the year.

The inner depths of the stone began to move and glow. It was as if the inside was melting, becoming liquid, a sea of glass filled with fire. That flaming nucleus grew and swelled until the stone was a soft, pulsing membrane in my hand, filled with swirling light. It flooded the garden with light, like an August noon, yet the brilliance of what I carried did not blind me. I held it high over my head, and it baked down on the barren twigs and stalks of the garden.

"That's right," Beryl said. "Now, enter."

Now was no time for doubt. I pulled the stone down and stared into it, willing it to let me enter it. I pressed it against my forehead, feeling it bend but not yield.

Did she mean "enter," literally?

I closed my eyes. I thought about the light, the liquid fire, swirling around inside the stone. I imagined that same purifying heat spreading over me, burning me without consuming.

I felt a hot bright flash of pain, followed by the most soothing sweetness, like twilight in the spring.

And, even though the stone still lay in my hand, I knew I was inside.

I opened my eyes and saw that we were still in the garden, surrounded by light, but otherwise nothing was different.

Except I was different. I felt light, weightless, as though I could lift up my arms and fly away like a bird, and yet, at the same time, compact, powerful, my limbs lithe and supple.

"Show me this garden on its most glorious day," Beryl said. "Nothing less than its best."

I gazed around at the lifeless scene.

"Well," I began, "the fountain used to work, and there were goldfish swimming in it."

A burst of china-blue water erupted from the fountains and leapt over the marble lovers. Splashing filled the garden theater with its soothing sound. I ran to the edge and saw a family of fat red and white carp flicking their tails through the rising water.

"And water lilies," I added. They bobbed to the surface as if they'd been waiting at the bottom for me.

My pulse quickened. I turned to look at Beryl. She nodded encouragingly.

I looked around. The garden existed in my memory, but where were its details? I felt blind, groping through the fog of my memory. "The yew trees were a bit more trimmed, I think." Each tree shook itself and dropped its dead excess until they all stood, stately and thick. I began to feel giddy.

"There were red roses along here, and pink and white ones there. Big as saucers, and oh! their scent." Each bush sprang to life as I spoke it into being, blossoms buxom, leaves thick and glossy, thorns curling out from the stalks like scimitars unsheathing. I stepped back, just in case.

How to describe this delicious power, this heady freedom, to speak life into being! Sunshine broke through the fog in my mind, and my own memories unfurled like these tender plants. With them came more than flowers, but feelings, snippets, whole mornings of pottering around these walks, teasing my puppy, doting on my mother.

"Over here were . . . peonies, I think." Lush pink and white blossoms opened on green stalks that rose from the ground. Those had been Mama's favorites. Blowsy and bold, like her.

I spun around. "I don't remember all the names. But there were violets and pansies and daffodils and tulips in every shade, all around here. And there were little trees that blossomed in the springtime. And honeysuckle, and morning glory." Wherever I pointed, shoots poked through the soft mold and uncurled heavenward; vines wrapped themselves around the Grecian columns and opened yellow and blue blossoms. The more I spoke, the more the light around us grew, and color and perfume filled the air. Bees and butterflies caught flecks of sunlight from no sun that I could see, but the light danced over them as if it were mid-morning.

"I'm afraid I've gotten this a bit muddled," I told Beryl. "I probably have everything blooming out of season."

"None of it blooms in winter anyway," she said, smiling. "You've done a wonderful job."

"Oh, but I'm not done," I said, my heart pounding. An idea had planted itself in my mind that refused to be brushed aside. "There was a little house, over here, with screens instead of walls. We often took our tea there." The house appeared, complete with chairs and a steaming tea service set on the table.

"And here on this bench," I said, through the lump in my throat, "was where Mama and Papa would sit in the evenings and talk."

I closed my eyes, squeezing them hard. Oh, please, please. I opened them slowly, so slowly that through the tangle of lashes I couldn't be sure of what I saw first, and almost didn't dare find out.

And still, when I saw, I didn't dare believe. Maybe desire had painted them in my mind, and they'd flicker away like dreams do when I wake suddenly.

But, no, they didn't vanish.

I opened my eyes, and my parents were there.

Chapter 29

No other sight in the garden was half so lovely.

Mama sat on the bench, her face upturned to Papa's. Papa's arm stretched out to slip a daisy behind Mama's ear. He looked a bit comical, concentrating on where to put the flower. At last he got it to stay without falling into her lap. She made a teasing face and pretended to return to her book and ignore him.

There they were, so alive, so real. I ran to embrace them.

"Wait," Beryl called.

I ignored her and flung out my arms to squeeze them both together. How surprised they'll be to see me now! "Mama! Papa!" I cried.

They didn't respond.

I halted just inches away from Mama and stretched out my hand to touch her cheek. My fingers buzzed and tingled.

Papa tried reading over Mama's shoulder, and she elbowed him good-naturedly.

Beryl appeared at my side. I hadn't heard her approach.

I did not turn. The pain in my chest wouldn't let me.

"I'm sorry," she said. "I should have thought to warn you."

I filled my eyes with the sight of them. So real, I could smell Mama's perfume. Their voices felt like ancient lullabies.

"I'm glad you didn't warn me."

She placed a hand on my shoulder. "It's best that you let them go now."

I closed my eyes. When I opened them, Mama and Papa were still there, talking quietly with each other. "Must I?"

"You're seeing a memory," Beryl said, "sweet as it is. But for your kind, memories of the dead are best seen through the cloudy glass of time and dreams."

In other words, not seen. Longed for, but unseen.

"There is nothing more I want to see." With a heavy heart, I said to my parents, "You aren't here anymore." They faded and vanished. Mama's book fell open on the bench.

"I'm sorry, Lucinda," she said. "I didn't mean to hurt you again."

The flowers that had enchanted me seemed drab and wretched now.

"You've done beautifully," Beryl said. "This garden reminds me of my home."

I sank down onto the garden bench. Mama and Papa

sitting, talking—the image hovered before my eyes, so real, so taunting. And yet, for all this fresh hurt, I would do it again. If Beryl's stone were mine, the temptation to do this every day would be irresistible.

Beryl sat beside me, watching me with concern. I wiped my eyes and blew out my breath. I needed something, anything else, to think about. An idea struck me.

"Beryl," I said, handing her the stone, "can you show me *your* home?"

She was reluctant to take the stone from my hand. "I . . . stopped doing this long ago," she said, slowly. "Many, many years ago. It was too painful."

I understood, too well. "Never mind," I said. "I'm sorry I asked."

She shook her head. "No. I want you to see." She reached for my hand and held it. Once again I felt the full sensation of her—living marble, breathing glass, cold and yet full of fire.

"Close your eyes," she said. I obeyed, and felt the sweep of heat and pain followed by blissful, dewy coolness, and the scent of spring blossoms.

"Open them," she said.

I opened my eyes.

◆ ◆ ◆

We stood on a mountaintop, overlooking a valley that stretched forever, with woods and pastures seemingly lit from within themselves. A river curled across the valley, and where it bent and ran off into the mountains, a city rose up as if carved from the ground itself. Its towers and walls shimmered with color and swayed gently in the wind, like trees.

No smoke rose into the sky. No filth ran out its water gates. No cemeteries dotted its hills.

The city was far from me, filled with many thousands of buildings, and the lands beyond it farther still, yet I could see it as clearly as if distance had no meaning. In all this vastness I could see every leaf, every berry, every pebble and fish in the bed of every stream.

In the city, children played in the streets, and adults rested and talked and worked among them. Some were reading, some teaching, some building and sculpting and making music. Animals of all kinds moved freely among the people—bears and wolves and badgers lolling on the ground where infants crawled, snakes draped lovingly over women's shoulders, falcons nibbling from girls' hands.

I turned to Beryl, and saw her for the first time.

My heart broke.

She met my gaze, then pointed beyond the city. I looked and saw another mountain, white as cotton. One face was hollowed to form a natural amphitheatre. On the grass inside the hollow stood a well of dark gray stones.

I remembered what she'd told me about banishment. "Is that . . . ?"

She nodded quickly.

I turned back toward more pleasant sights.

I could have stayed in that illusion forever, but Beryl was suffering.

"Shall we go back?" I asked.

Beryl hung her head. It was, for her, an unanswerable dilemma.

I reached for her hand. "I'll be with you." I said. What weak comfort I must be to someone born in this paradise!

She squeezed my hand, closed her eyes, and reached for her stone.

A voice called to us.

Beryl's eyes flew open.

Five people ran toward us, ascending the mountain as easily as I might run down a grassy slope. I looked at Beryl. She stood transfixed, watching them, clutching the stone at her throat.

I couldn't understand it. Unlike my parents, these people saw us. They were calling and waving. Three women, I saw, and two men, calling to Beryl, with a word I did not understand, nor could I repeat it, though I tried. My mouth could not form it.

"Aren't we only seeing your memory?" I whispered.

Beryl stood trembling, reaching out to them. "I thought so," she whispered back.

And they were upon us like stampeding cattle, attacking her with kisses and astonished laughter. And tears.

They were her family.

Was it real? I thought she couldn't go back. I thought—
she thought—she was barred forever. Was this only a
dream, like my dreams that turned to nightmares when I
would wake and find my parents still gone?

I felt out of place, a gross intruder, not even the right
kind of creature. I backed away, but Beryl reached for me
and pulled me close.

"Lucinda," she said, her face shining, "this is my family."
Turning to them, she said, in words I could understand,
"This is Lucinda, my dearest friend."

A woman stepped forward and embraced me. The others, each in turn, did the same, smiling warmly. I felt kindness and welcome flow from them into me. Then, like
moths to a flame, they flocked back to Beryl, to pet her and
convince themselves she was truly there. Her two sisters
linked arms with her and began leading her down the trail
with them toward the city.

I hesitated. Beryl turned back. She pulled away from
her sisters and came back to me.

"It's all right," she said. "We'll leave now and go back to
the garden."

I had a terrible choice to make. But really, it was no
choice at all.

"We?" I said. "Not 'we.' You stay."

Beryl shook her head. "I can't leave you defenseless. I'll
only say good-bye to them."

"You won't," I said. "You've come back home. Whatever barred you before is gone. You mustn't leave."

She gripped my arms tightly, at war with herself.

A thought struck me. "You apologized, Beryl. You went to Aunt with an offering, and told her the truth, and how sorry you were. How your heart was broken by it. That took courage."

She shook her head vehemently. "It doesn't bring John back," she said. "It doesn't fix your aunt's broken life. That couldn't be enough."

"It was all you could do," I said. And in that moment, I knew it was true. "All you can do is enough."

Below us, on the sides of the mountain, grasses and trees swayed gently, as if bidding Beryl welcome. Her family stood at a respectful distance, watching but not interfering.

"I wouldn't leave, if it were me," I said. "At least one of us should have her family." I kissed her forehead. "I'll be all right. I'll go where Coxley can't find me." I realized something surprising. "After seeing all this, I feel I can do anything."

She threw her arms around my neck. "Bless you, Lucinda," she said. "Bless you forever." She pulled back and looked at me once more, her smile shining. Then she pulled the net that carried her stone off of her neck. "Take this with you," she said. I started to protest, but she silenced me. "I can forge another. Take this to remember me by, and to protect yourself."

I took the stone from her hand. "You said it was your soul."

"I'm not who I was when I left this place," she said. "Take this, and my soul and I will make ourselves new." She draped the netting around my neck. "You know what to do," she said. She kissed my cheek. "Good-bye, dear friend."

She would be happy at last. How could I not be glad? "Good-bye, Beryl."

Her family stood some distance off, watching. She turned toward them, and they beckoned to her. She took a step toward them, then looked back at me.

"Lucinda," she said. "When you get home, look in the tower room. There's a present for you in the telescope."

I nodded and waved.

Beryl halted halfway between me and her family. I had to leave for her sake.

Light, I told the stone, and it burst with effortless radiance. It, too, was home. I closed my eyes and willed myself inside it. Back to the garden, I told it. Take *me* home.

Chapter 30

I opened my eyes to cold and darkness. It was the moon-lit garden at midnight, and Dog had found me. He nibbled on dried flower stalks.

After the lush heat of Beryl's world, I couldn't endure the cold. I ran for the house, with Dog at my heels and Beryl's stone thumping my breastbone at each step. Once inside I lit a candle from warm embers in the parlor fire, then threw a few more logs on. Before long, flames sprouted up, probing their way around the wood.

I stared at the fire, at the blank spaces on the wall where Beryl's paintings had been. A wave of loneliness hit me. To drive it away I took a candle and found my way to the tower room in search of my gift.

There was the humpback telescope under its leather wrap. I looked all around it, and the open case lying on the floor, for some type of gift, and saw nothing. So I unscrewed the eyepiece and peered through the telescope at the moon. Something blocked the view. I swiveled the telescope around and reached inside. Resting against the lens was a fabric pouch. I tipped it into my hand, and out poured a cascade of colored stones.

River pebbles from paradise. Worth a sultan's fortune here.

I poured the stones back in and lay the pouch on the floor. It didn't matter to me now.

I looked out the windows at the grounds of the Palisades, and the view of the city and the dark sea beyond. Torches in the highest towers of Sebastien Palace winked like fireflies. Everything else was dark.

A pinpoint of light appeared through the trees and was gone. It appeared again, moving toward me, up the road from the bridge into the city.

Something told me it wasn't harmless. My tongue felt dry in my mouth.

I swiveled the old telescope in the direction of the light and aimed as best I could. It creaked on its axle, but when I peered through the eyepiece and adjusted the dials, it soon found its focus.

A disembodied head floated toward me. It was a rider carrying a torch that only illuminated his face.

He came closer. I saw that he wore no cloak or overcoat. His pale hair gleamed by torchlight. So did the golden epaulets on his shoulders.

Chapter 31

I dropped down onto the floor. All I could do was breathe.

I'll go where he can't find me, I'd said. That's all right, Beryl, go be with your family here in your heaven-world, and leave me alone with a devil in mine. I insist.

Mother of God.

I wrapped my fingers around the stone at my throat and willed it to make me still and silent. If I stayed here, lay quiet on the dark floor, threw the telescope's leather cloak over me, would he think the house abandoned and move on?

I thought not.

If I gave him the prize I held in my hands, would he go away and leave me alone?

Not a prayer of it.

And if he got the stone from me, as he surely would,

after he killed me, what would he do with its power? As powerful as he was now, Chief Minister of Justice, I knew that was not enough for him. What would he do to Gregor, the future king?

He would tear through the house until he found me, I knew. My only hope was to get out of the house before he did. And here I was, trapped in a tower like the girl in the tale with the long, long hair.

I stood up, moving as softly as I could, and fumbled at the latch of the nearest window. It swung open on squealing hinges. I paused to see if Coxley had heard, but all I heard downstairs was smashing glass.

I leaned out the window and looked down. It was a full story drop to the roof below the tower. From there the roof sloped down to a single-story drop into thick evergreen bushes. If I could survive the first drop without breaking both my legs, I might be able to tumble to safety and run away. *If* Coxley didn't hear or see me.

A horrific crash followed by ringing notes told me Coxley had annihilated the piano in the ballroom. Why, why would he do that? Did he think I would hide inside it? Was this his revenge on Beryl? On me?

Wind pummeled me, whipping my hair out of its setting. Perhaps its noise would conceal me. The drop seemed endless in the darkness, but crashing glass below was more fearsome. Jump, now, some good angel whispered in my ear, and I obeyed before I could think. I clambered up on a chair, gripped the upper sill, and hoisted my legs out. My slippers fell off my feet. I leaped forward.

For an instant I lay in the hand of God. Then I landed on the roof, smashing my knees and rolling to the very edge before catching a grip on the slates. I let myself fall into the thorny bushes, and dangled there, trying to catch my breath, my eyes screwed shut, every bit of me scratched and bruised and stinging.

From out here I couldn't hear Coxley's rampages, so I didn't know whether or not they'd stopped. I flexed my ankles and wrists. It appeared that my body still worked. I clawed my way out of the deep shrubs, suffering several more gashes, a ripped-off sleeve, and a tear in my skirt before landing on the ground.

Each step was painful, but I forced myself to run across the dark lawns, sidestepping the drive and aiming directly for the road.

The wind chilled me. It lashed my face, flinging grit into my eyes. I closed my eyes, and dangling branches whipped me. My lungs ached, and my empty belly stabbed with pain.

"*Meh-heh-heh!*"

Dog galloped along beside me.

I couldn't see him, but I heard and felt him bash against my shins. I was so glad for his company, until Coxley's horse neighed, a shrill, piercing cry, and the door of the house slammed.

"*Gyup,*" I heard him call out.

And galloping hoofbeats were after us.

I reached the road and crossed it. The frozen grass of the margin was easier on my bare feet. I hoped I could disappear in the shadow of the ditch.

I stumbled and fell. My knees wouldn't let me get up.

I lay praying, clutching my hands around brambles and weeds, wishing the ground would swallow me. Beryl's stone, just under my neck, pressed into my windpipe.

The horse tore through the hedge and clattered across the road. With a cry from Coxley, it leaped across the ditch, sailing just over me, and landed in a farmer's field.

In the dark, under the cover of my body, I tore the stone from my throat and scrabbled in the frozen dirt with my fingers, trying to bury it.

I didn't get far. A stinging whip wrapped itself around my arm, yanking it up and out from under me. The stone fell. I prayed he hadn't seen it.

The whip relaxed and fell off my arm. I forced myself to rise from the dirt and face him, shivering with cold and pain and dread.

Here is where I die, I told myself.

Coxley sat astride his huge beast, moonlight gleaming on his leather boots. Even in the winter night, I felt cold waves of malice rolling off him that chilled me far more than the wind. His pale, bloodless cheeks were hollow, sucked in, like withered dead skin over bones. Only his epaulets, and his crystal blue eyes, had any color at all.

Behind him, in the farmer's field, hollow stumps of mown cornstalks became breathy reeds, sighing and rattling in the wind. His stallion snorted and shook his harnesses.

From out of nowhere, Dog appeared, charging into the horse's knees. The stallion reared angrily, pawing the air. Dog rammed him again with no regard for the horse's kicking legs.

"No, Dog!" I cried. "Stop it! Run away!"

Coxley shouted at his horse to stand. There was a loud crack, and Coxley's whip wrapped itself around Dog's neck. With a mighty heave, Coxley flung Dog's body high in the air, his body twisting and kicking.

He landed with a thump and lay still.

Chapter 32

Coxley reined his horse close, his whip handle clenched in his gloved hand. I turned away, waiting for him to strike.

Instead he grabbed my arm and hauled me effortlessly across the pommel of his saddle. Striking his horse on the flank, he spurred him back toward the house.

Each bounce of the saddle sent the pommel pounding into my belly. I couldn't help touching Coxley, smelling the wool of his uniform, feeling his cold iron form. I nearly retched.

I mourned for Dog.

He dumped me off the horse, and I landed on the gravel drive before the house. I could barely feel my feet, frozen in their shredded stockings.

Coxley dismounted and picked up the guttering torch that he must have dropped there when he chased after me.

Its flames resurrected, and he held it near my face until I shrank back.

"Where is she?" he said.

"Gone," I said.

"Gone where?"

I tilted my chin up and looked at the stars in the sky. How could they shine on a night like this?

"Gone where you can't go," I told him.

For a moment I saw fear in his eyes, before it turned to anger. He shoved the torch closer until my cheek hurt. "Where is her stone?"

I hesitated. I saw a way. "Gone with her," I said.

He jabbed with the torch. "You lie."

He stared at me, as if his gaze alone would crumble me. It might have.

"How do I lie?" I demanded. "How would she have left this world without it?"

He spoke. "Your lie is written on your lips. You can't deceive me."

He meant it. I knew it. What to do now? I rubbed my arms and tried to think.

"Cold?" Coxley said. "Let me warm you." He climbed back into the saddle, nudged his horse toward the house and dangled the torch in the midst of a bare-branched shrub.

The bush caught fire. Orange feathers ruffled along its spiny branches slowly, almost lovingly. Fire spread through the bush—a woodsy scent, a cheerful crackle.

"Where is the stone?" Coxley shouted. He ambled his horse toward another bush.

The wind fanned the flame from the first bush until it lapped at a windowsill. No. Please no. The second bush began to gleam red.

I stood, with effort. Should I run? If I reached the stone, could I use it in some way?

The windowsill was burning. The fire threw dancing orange stripes upon the inside wall. It was the ballroom. Glass began to shatter, and the drapes lit with a whoosh.

Coxley tossed his torch inside the house, then came back to where I huddled. He dismounted and pulled a dagger from its sheath. He pressed its tip gently into my belly.

"Whether or not you tell me where the stone is, I will find it," he said. "You can make this less painful by helping me."

Fire had spread to envelop the first floor. Light was already beginning to dance on a second-floor ceiling.

Courage, Lucinda. "You won't find it," I said, "and I won't help you."

"Very well," he said, and pressed the dagger in.

"No, stop," I cried.

"Yes?"

Cinders flew high as if ascending to heaven behind him.

"The stone is . . ."

What could I say? I looked at the burning ballroom, and thought of Gregor. Had a thousand things been different, I might have danced with him there in that room. How could I betray him by arming Coxley with Beryl's stone?

She gave it to *me*.

I stood as tall as I could. "You killed my parents," I said. "You killed my little goat. It may be that you'll kill me, too, but I won't surrender to fearing you. And I won't give you Beryl's stone."

Coxley stared at me with hatred clamped between his teeth. Behind him, an inferno raged. Its rushing groan filled my ears. Every breath burned my lungs.

"Your parents died slowly, did anyone tell you that?" he said. "I watched them. Your father watched your mother bleed, and there was nothing he could do. His legs didn't work anymore. A miserable sight. Even for my tastes."

The rushing black shock that filled my ears drowned out the roar of the fire. I saw in my mind my parents' last moments. My bruised knees buckled under me. Coxley raised me to my feet again, a cruel mockery of gentle manners.

"I think your end should mirror theirs," he said. "Don't you?"

He took my hand and overturned it gently. With the tip of his dagger, he drew a delicate curve across my wrist.

I could barely feel it. Beads of blood rose from the wound, and in another heartbeat, spouted out.

I watched the dark river splashing on the stones at my feet. My blood soiled Coxley's brass buttons. A wrinkle of irritation crossed his lips. He wiped himself and his dagger with a kerchief, sheathed the blade, and remounted his horse.

"It won't be long," he said. "You'll go to sleep. I was softer than I needed to be."

My knees buckled once more, and I sank to the ground. Blazing rafters from the highest roofs caved in up themselves, sending jets of orange sparks, like prayers, into the night.

Soon I would be with my parents.

Coxley placed a shiny boot into his stirrup. A sudden sound rising above the fire's howl made us both turn, just in time to see Dog barrel both horns into Coxley's other leg, upending him.

"Dog!" I called. "You're alive!"

He ran to me and dropped something hard and wet from his mouth into my sagging skirt. I reached for him, wanting to be sure he wasn't a ghost. His nostrils flared at the puddle of blood on the ground. Then he charged Coxley once more.

The first crash had knocked Coxley on his back, with one leg horribly twisted and stuck in the high stirrup. A mortal man would have broken his back, but Coxley, snorting with rage, was only inconvenienced.

The sight of Dog bounding over the frozen ground filled me with new hope. If he could survive, perhaps I could. I raised my arm high and squeezed the wound tight with my other hand.

Dog ran underneath the stallion's belly, which spooked him, making him rear on his hind legs. Coxley dangled like a rag doll, his yellow hair dragging in the dirt. He shrieked curses at the horse and at Dog.

Dog rammed the horse's hind legs, and the stallion leaped forward, dragging Coxley across the drive.

I looked down in my skirt. Dog had brought me Beryl's stone.

What could I do with it? I didn't have Beryl's power. Could I, at least, use it to send a message?

My bleeding had slowed. I stared at the stone. Light, I demanded it. Light for dear life. For *my* dear life, even if it's only dear to me.

The stone blazed like a beacon.

The stallion screamed. Coxley had freed himself and was beating the horse with his whip handle. Poor beast.

With all the effort I could muster, I quieted my mind, thought about Beryl's world, and entered the stone.

I opened my eyes, but saw only as I might through a dark and dirty window. I saw people in the distance, not clearly enough to make them out. "Beryl," I called, "Beryl, where are you? Come help me!"

A figure ran toward me but was held away by the hazy barrier. "Tell Beryl that Lucinda needs her," I called. "Please!"

And the vision, or illusion, if that's what it was, ended. Coxley snatched the stone from my lap.

Chapter 33

I abandoned all thought of my wrist. I backed away from Coxley. He held his dagger high and scanned the firelit lawns searching for Dog.

Run, Doggy Goat, I called to him silently. *Run away!*

But Dog brayed loudly, a battle cry, and galloped once more toward Coxley.

Coxley flung his knife.

And the heavens opened.

Blinding white cascaded down in a circle around me and Coxley. Shooting stars began tumbling onto the ground around us.

They weren't stars. They were Beryl's people.

And Coxley recognized them.

He held his stone—my stone, Beryl's stone—high in the air and began shouting strange words. The stone shone green and red. Waves of nausea and pain washed over me, and I vomited on the ground, in the presence of angels. He was using the stone as a weapon to kill me faster.

Dozen of bright people came. Strong arms reached around me and pulled me to safety, and I looked up into Beryl's face. She wrapped her fingers around my wrist, and I felt my flesh knit back together.

"It's all right," she told me.

"What are you going to do?" I whispered.

"Watch."

I was outside of the circle now. It tightened around Coxley like a noose, several people deep. Each wore a stone around their necks, and they glowed yellow, sending a golden halo of light up into the sky.

Still Coxley held his angry red stone high and screamed and howled his strange words. With each one I felt crippling jabs of pain in my belly. *Hurry*, I prayed.

The halo condensed itself around Coxley. A tourniquet of light.

With an agonizing scream, Coxley let go of Beryl's stone. It flew high in the air and landed in Beryl's hand.

The band of light became a cylinder around him. He thrashed and clawed against it. It solidified and took shape.

It became a well of stones.

Coxley's cool blue eyes became torches of fury. He slashed with his fingernails at his black clothing until it fell off in shreds. The well held his legs and his trunk, but his chalk-white arms pounded against the sides.

A woman in the circle spoke a question. I didn't know the words, but it became clear from how they all looked around at each other that she had asked for a volunteer.

No one spoke.

Coxley laughed.

I remembered what Beryl had said. "It takes another to go with them, to force them down the well, making sure their banishment succeeds." A horrible, sick feeling came over me. Why would any of these majestic people do such a thing? Why should they?

Beryl stepped forward. "I brought the stone here," she cried. "I'm the reason Lucinda is in danger. I'll go."

No!

Murmurs ran through the circle. I recognized her family members, protesting.

Coxley flexed his arms and laughed.

Beryl fell to her knees and pleaded with them. "For Lucinda's sake, I beg you, let me go."

No, no, no. Oh, Beryl, go home. Don't sacrifice yourself for me after waiting so long, after seeing their loving faces. There *must* be some other way.

"This burden is mine," Beryl insisted. "Send me now."

Her parents and sisters steeled their devastated faces. Beryl approached Coxley and locked her arms around him, still clutching her stone. His muscles quivered with effort as he pushed against her.

"Quickly!" she gasped.

"*No!*" I cried.

All the stones flashed gold and orange, like the fire behind them. Without any pause, Beryl vaulted the wall of the narrow well, still gripping her writhing prisoner. They disappeared.

Crying aloud in anguish, Beryl's family and all the rest vanished like popping soap bubbles.

It was over.

My body shuddered. It was over. And Beryl was gone.

My eyes flooded with tears.

So I almost didn't notice when a hand appeared over the lip of the well. A broad, long-fingered white hand, followed by another.

I was paralyzed. I could only watch as Coxley pulled his head up and leered at me. No more was he the precise, urbane Lord Minister of Justice. Now he was truly diabolical. Such malice, such triumph in his eyes, and now all my help was gone.

A clatter of hoofbeats rang out from the drive, and a rider galloped into view through the clouds of smoke. It was Gregor. He reigned in his horse, surveying the wreckage. "Lucinda!"

Coxley had both arms over the edge and was hoisting his body up with difficulty. Beryl, I saw, still clung to his side, her arms around his chest.

I ran to the well. Coxley snarled and hissed at Beryl.

Then, from nowhere, a small brown billy goat sprang from his hind legs and butted Coxley hard on the side of his head.

It made a marvelous cracking sound.

Coxley fell with a scream, catching himself only by his fingertips.

Dog, standing on two legs, trampled upon his hands.

The wail of someone falling echoed up from far, far down into the well.

Dog trotted over to me and hunkered down at my feet. *"Meh-heh-heh!"*

Chapter 34

Gregor slid off his saddle and ran to me.

I blinked at him, swaying.

He turned me by the shoulders so I faced the fire and used its light to inspect me. "You're hurt!" He fished a handkerchief from his pocket and wiped my face. Then he discovered the blood soaked into my dress. "We have to get you to a doctor," he cried, and he picked me up like a sack of oats.

"Put me *down*," I said. I realized how harsh I sounded. "I was bleeding, but I'm not anymore." That's when I saw the red flower that dangled from his hand. Mine, from the ball. A thousand years ago.

He set me down. "Are you all right?" He threw his coat around my shoulders.

My dress was in tatters. I pulled the coat tight.

His anxious eyes scanned my face, probably covered

with blood and ashes. "What happened here?" he said. "Who did this to you?"

I shook my head. I couldn't tell the tale. Not now.

His eyes swept the wreckage. I followed his gaze to where Coxley had vanished. I saw only Dog standing on a patch of undisturbed gravel, nosing the ground.

"Lucinda," he said, "who *did* this? Where are they now?"

What I'd have given to cling to his arm. I could barely stand. "It was the same person who tried to rob you last night," I said. "He's gone now, forever."

"Dead?"

I shook my head. "Gone." And so was Beryl. "Why are you here?" The words blurted out before I could stop them.

Gregor looked deflated. "I wanted to speak with you."

My body felt heavy and stiff, each bruise making its presence known. "I'm sorry about coming to the ball," I said. "It wasn't my idea." And that was only half a lie.

He waved this away. "No matter."

Indeed. What did it matter now?

I pulled his coat closer around me and watched the fire. One corner of the stone structure still stood as before, but most of the walls had collapsed. The flames burned low.

"I've come to take you home," Gregor said.

"I am home." I felt a bitter laugh rise in my dry throat.

Gregor kicked at a smoking piece of charred wood. "Peter told me where you'd be."

It felt as though he spoke from miles away. Only a fragment of his voice could find me; only a fragment of my mind could hear.

"So he didn't escape the palace, I take it," I said. I couldn't worry about Peter. But perhaps some ladylike gratitude was called for. "It was kind of him to think of me."

"It wasn't him, it was me," Gregor said, indignant. "And no, he certainly didn't 'escape,' as you put it. I asked him where you were. I drove out to find you, and when I saw the flames, I took one of the horses and rode on ahead."

Something told the numb part of my mind that this ought to impress me. "Oh?"

Gregor seemed dissatisfied with my lack of feeling.

I was so bone-weary, each word was torturous. "It's all right, Gregor. It was kind of you to rescue me, but you can go back now. I'll give you no more worry. I know that's what you came to ask of me. I won't come near you or the princess again."

Gregor was vexed now. "What does this have to do with the princess?" He swept his arm across what had been the Palisades. "You're stunned by what's happened. When the carriage comes, I'm taking you home."

His good heart would be gallant to the end, but I needed to end this. I couldn't, after all I'd gone through, let *my* heart be broken again.

I slipped off the coat and handed it back to him. "*Prince*

Gregor," I said, "there's no place for me in your world. I won't try to create one."

Firelight wavered over his face. His lips moved, as though he couldn't choose his words.

"You won't?"

I shook my head. Smoke filled my eyes. "We saw tonight what a disaster it is every time I try."

Gregor's face contorted with some emotion that I could not read. My own emotions were more than I could manage as it was.

The royal coach swept into view around the curve of the driveway and halted with a jingle of harnesses and livery. The driver jumped down and ran toward us, his face full of alarm. Gregor nodded to reassure him, and he led Gregor's horse back to the team.

Gregor turned to me, his face tight. "You need, at the least, a change of clothes, some rest, and food. I can avoid you completely once we're there."

Rest. Food. Avoid you. How was it that I still had room for more pain? "Perhaps that would be best."

I let him escort me to the carriage. As we drove away I pressed my face to the glass and stared at the ruin of my hopes.

Gregor jumped out when we arrived and handed me off to a housekeeper, instructing her to see to my needs. Then he bowed, turned on his heel, and strode off in the other direction.

Mercifully, the good woman said little as she helped me out of my silk rags, washed me, and bundled me into a nightgown. She didn't even allow her face to comment. Another servant kindled a fire while she led me to bed, and I accepted their ministrations without question. The blankets were heavy, the pillows deep, the darkness soft and protective. I went straightaway to sleep.

Chapter 35

Squealing hinges woke me. I sat up in bed in a panic.

Morning sun streamed through ice-edged windows, illuminating a magnificent room bedecked with gold—gold curtains, tapestries, covers.

I searched for the source of the noise. The door to the room hovered open, and poking inside like a snapping turtle's was the priceless face of Princess Beatrix.

"Oh good! You're up." She opened the door and pranced in with two of her ladies in tow.

I yanked the covers up to my chin and rubbed a hand over my face. Had I washed it last night? I couldn't remember.

"We're here to see about gowns," she informed me, perching on the edge of my bed. "Marie, here, is probably about your size, or if not, then possibly Celeste." She gestured to the two blushing girls, obviously sisters, who towered behind her. Marie was nearly six feet tall, and Celeste, definitely an inch or two over that.

"Ah, um, that's more than kind of you," I said, inching backward on my buttocks.

Princess Beatrix flopped forward until she was lying beside me, her face propped on her hands. "You certainly look different without that ridiculous mask," she said. "Not a pox mark to be seen. Such vanity!"

"Sorry," I said lamely.

She popped upright and snatched my covers off me. "Up with you, morning's wasting. You've already missed breakfast." She pulled me bodily from the bed. My feet froze on the flagstones. My knees wobbled, my muscles moaned.

Princess Beatrix stood with both hands on her hips. "This won't do," she said, frowning. "Marie's half a head taller than you. Both of you, run and fetch Louise." The blushing girls were quick to oblige.

I collapsed backward onto the bed.

Beatrix located an armoire and wrestled it open, flicking through the clothing inside.

"Ugh! What is this? Cobwebs and rags." She paused to glance over at me. "Gregor's told me what a special friend you are to him," she said. "So I'm sure you and I will get on famously. Gregor's such a dear soul."

I bit my tongue. So she'd come to flaunt her intimacy with Gregor. I could withstand it for one morning. I had no need to bare my feelings to her.

Beatrix dropped a few wads of fabric on the bed beside me. "Try these on. Bit stiff, don't you think?"

I poked at the petticoat she'd given me, confused. "I don't think so, do you?"

Her laugh trilled up to the ceiling. "I don't mean that, I mean Gregor!"

This was so unexpected, I had no clever response. "Stiff?"

"As a log. What kind of husband will that make him, I wonder?" She waggled her eyebrows mischievously.

So much for my self-control. My face grew hot.

"Here's Louise," she said as the door opened. I was made to stand next to Louise, and after Beatrix declared that we could have been twins, and several runs back to Louise's trunks were made, I was outfitted in a handsome green velvet dress. Her ladies attacked me with hairbrushes and hand creams and stockings until I was deemed presentable.

"You really have no need for a mask," Beatrix said generously.

I curtsyed.

"I must fly," she said, shooing her ladies out the door. "So glad you'll be here to help with the wedding, now that it's been moved up to Christmas Eve."

Self-control. "It has?"

"My prince could hardly wait another day," she said.

"Who can blame him?" I said.

✦   ✦   ✦

I sat in my room, leafing through the pages of a book I found without seeing any of the words. Images of burning rubble scrolled endlessly before my eyes.

Only the faintest scar remained on my wrist. I was glad it was there. A lifelong reminder.

A servant knocked at my door to tell me luncheon was being served in the dining room, and I was invited to join the royal family. This horrifying notion banished any thoughts of food. I sat for another hour and listened to my stomach growl, wondering what would become of Beryl.

The more I tried not to think of food, the more desperately hungry I became. At last I decided that the danger must be past, and I ventured out the door and down the corridor toward the stairs. From the savory smells, the dining room wasn't hard to locate. I crossed the threshold into the opulent room and stopped in my tracks. Gregor sat alone at one end of a long table, fiddling with the handle of a teacup. At the sight of me, he stood, bowed, and left the room another way.

I slid into a chair, numb. Around the room a parade of marble bas-relief warriors jousted, shot arrows, and threw javelins in a never-ending battle. Only the fallen warriors with their lolling mouths and slits for eyes would ever rest.

◆ ◆ ◆

They brought me a plate of food. I picked at it, barely able to swallow. I needed to leave this place. *"Eat,"* I scolded myself. Gather all the strength you can, then leave and go . . . where? Back to the ruin of my house. I could sleep in the barns with Dog to keep me warm. It would do for a day or two until I'd had time to think of something. Dog! Bless his loyal hide, he had more lives than a cat. The sight of him landing after Coxley threw him would haunt me long after this.

I forced down my meal, rose from the table, and hurried back upstairs. Once in the corridor I hesitated, unsure of which room was mine. I lingered for a moment, waiting for someone to pass by who could tell me, but no one came. I paced up and down, analyzing each door until I'd convinced myself it was one in particular. I rattled its doorknob and, hearing no response, opened the door.

There stood Peter, shirtless and in his knickers, a tailor measuring his outstretched arms.

"Oh!" I quickly pulled the door shut.

Peter?

"Lucinda!" Peter's voice called after me. "Come in."

What was he *doing* here? What was he doing *here*? And in his knickers?

"Not till you're dressed," I said through the crack.

Peter made a noise of annoyance. He and the tailor exchanged some words. The door opened and the tailor breezed out, wrinkling his nose at me. I wasn't sure whether it was me, personally, or Louise's dress that he found so objectionable.

I pushed open the door. There sat Peter, lounging in an easy chair. He was clad in a lacy white shirt that was open to his chest, loose trousers, and a pair of embroidered red slippers.

"There you are!" Peter said pleasantly. He rose and kissed my hand.

I nodded. "Here *I* am. Why in the name of heaven are *you* here? And what's this about?" I indicated the hand he'd kissed.

He shrugged. "When in Rome, eh? Got to play the part. This is living, isn't it?"

I slid into a chair opposite him. "Not for me."

His face fell. "So Gregor's talked to you?"

I nodded. "Briefly."

Peter stretched his arms and propped both hands behind his head. "Short and to the point? Just as well."

I couldn't find any meaning in this utterance, and I didn't strain myself trying to. "Tell me, Peter, what fantastic yarn did you spin them to let you stay in the palace?"

He flicked a speck of dust from his trousers. "No yarn at all. Straight truth."

I leaned back against my chair. If I waited, sooner or later the details would brag their way out.

"Something I've been wondering, Peter," I said. "Were Beatrix's pearls really fake?"

He grinned. "How should I know? Always make people question the worth of their valuables. They stop guarding them so well, and don't work so hard to recover them."

I almost laughed. It would be some time before I could be merry again.

Peter watched me for a moment. Concern crossed his face.

"Say," he said, "you're not upset about Beatrix, are you?"

Why this sudden concern for my feelings? I wondered. And why did he need to remind me of her?

"No," I said cautiously. "Why should I . . . ?"

"Because I do like you, you know," Peter cut me off. "I mean, you've grown on me."

My mouth hung open.

"At first I thought you were just another stop on my rounds," he said, warming to his theme. "Place to sleep, make a lift, not get turned in. But I give you credit." He nodded solemnly. "You're hard to fool."

Perhaps when Coxley threw me off his horse I hit my head in a bad way.

"And you've cleaned up nice."

I explored my skull with my fingertips, looking for tender spots. "Why do you say this?"

"I just hate to disappoint a lady, is all," he said primly.

I worked hard not to grimace. "I'll survive."

He waved his hand at me. "And you see, that's the thing right there," he said. "I couldn't disappoint Beatrix, either. And if it came to a choice between the two of you, well . . ." His eyes were confident I'd sanction his choice. "You're a sight too independent minded, if you know what I mean.

But Beatrix—she's as gentle and tractable as a flower. That's the kind of woman you want."

I nodded sympathetically. "Absolutely."

He must have been tippling after breakfast. He'd probably robbed the wine cellars. What on earth did he mean, pitying me? What was he babbling about? I hid a smile at his depiction of Princess Beatrix, the gentle flower. Not as I knew her.

"Oh! By the by, I nearly forgot." Peter jumped from his chair and went to the bureau by his bed. He pulled open a drawer. "Gregor told me this morning about your house. I thought you might want to have this." He handed me a soft parcel wrapped in tissue paper. "Seeing as how I won't have a use for it anymore."

I only half heeded him. I took the parcel and wiped away the wrapping. Inside a discolored velvet pouch were a handful of papers. One was a sketch of Papa and Mama, and the other was a sketch of Mama and Papa holding a dark-haired child on their laps. Mama's drawings.

The last paper bore a red seal and ornate penmanship. "It's their will," I cried. "However did you find it?"

Peter grinned. "Behind the second wall panel to the right of the fireplace in the parlor. People always hide things there. I thought it would be a treasure map to the location of your parents' hidden fortune. No such luck."

I stroked the papers and pressed them to my heart.

Then I smiled and reached for his hand. "Thank you, Peter. If you weren't so rotten, I'd have nothing to remember my parents by."

He flopped back into his chair, his arms sprawling over its back. "It's the least I could do, after . . . you know."

My curiosity got the best of me. "No. I don't know. What are you talking about?"

He leaned forward in his chair. "You mean you truly don't know?"

I spread my hands wide. "Know what?"

He drummed his fingertips on the armrests of his chair. "The Crown Prince marries Princess Beatrix on Christmas Eve," he said.

Must everyone remind me? "I know that already. What about it?"

Peter's face went slightly pale. "You're looking at him."

◆ ◆ ◆

The story tumbled out. King Hubert and Queen Rosamond had two sons a year apart. When the elder son was three years old, he toddled off at the Winter Festival and was never found. As it happened, the Amaranth Witch had just appeared in Saint Laurenz for the first time when the queen was expecting her eldest, so afterward her strange appearance and the disappearance of the boy were linked and called the work of a curse.

The entire kingdom was searched. Soldiers looked for a

child with a long birthmark on his cheek. But in all the homes of the city he was never found, and so it was feared that he'd wandered into the river and been washed out to sea.

But then Queen Rosamond recognized his birthmark at the ball. King Hubert was so delighted that his son had amassed an independent fortune entirely on his own, he declared this to be the kind of king the country needed. Not a moony-eyed dreamer like Gregor. Before an astonished crowd of onlookers, King Hubert proclaimed Peter, né Roderick Alphonse, his rightful son and heir to the throne. Apparently Peter was nearly swallowed by a horde of young ladies eager to . . . congratulate him. Beatrix, not to be robbed of her kingdom, promptly switched her affections to Prince Roderick, and urged that the wedding be moved closer, for fear of her slippery new bridegroom changing his mind.

"But I did consider you," Peter assured me. "For quite a while. About half an hour. Beatrix wasn't too happy with me."

I covered my mouth with my hand. "I'm touched, Peter. Deeply."

He nodded, pleased with himself. I had to look away so he couldn't see me laugh.

"Where did you go, that day you got lost as a child?" I asked.

"I don't remember it," Peter said.

"Someone must have taken you in," I insisted.

Peter grinned. "Poke."

"What?"

"Poke, the peg-leg," he said. "I wandered into his little basement quarters, or so he tells me, and there I stayed. So he kept me on and fed me. Taught me all sorts of things. Before he lost his leg, he was the best thief this city'd ever seen."

"How'd he lose his leg?"

"Fellow hired him to scare some horses off a road at night," Peter said. "Man swore the carriage would be empty, and the driver, who was in on the plot, would jump to safety. No one'd get hurt." Peter shook his head. "But the carriage wasn't empty. A man and his wife died. Poke got his leg smashed. Always said later, that was his punishment. After that he stuck with good, honest thieving."

I nodded. I couldn't speak.

Peter watched me. "Here, now, don't take it so hard," he said, patting my hand.

I shook my head and wiped my eyes. "I'm not crying over you, silly."

Peter shook his head, plainly convinced otherwise. He patted my shoulder as he rose to show me out. "You should talk to Gregor," he said. "Losing Beatrix like that was a heavy blow. Maybe you could cheer him up."

◆　◆　◆

Somehow my feet led me down the corridor and stairs to the front door, not without passing a dozen servants busily decorating cut trees with apples and pomegranates and garlands of red ribbon. A doorman let me pass through and out into the grounds.

It felt less cold today than it had all the last week. The sky was gray, so thick it was nearly white. The kind of day that makes no shadows but bathes all the world in the same wan light.

I meandered down the walk, around the castle, and through the gardens. Evergreen boughs rustled as squirrels leaped among them, sending forth their piney fragrance. Red berries on an evergreen shrub couldn't have fit the Christmas wedding any better if Beatrix had ordered them herself.

I felt grateful for the cold. It reminded me of what was real.

So, swaggering, swindling Peter was king-to-be. A pickpocket in the palace. And spun-sugar Beatrix would be his wife. I smiled. At least she would not be quite the docile female Peter was expecting. May she live long and hearty.

I reached the rear of the palace. Is this where I was headed all along?

I looked up at the balcony. His balcony.

I gathered my courage.

As the first fleecy snowflakes began spiraling down from the sky, I bent to pick up a handful of stones.

They clattered onto the balcony floor. The curtain parted, and Gregor opened the door, his arms bare, his shirt open at the throat.

A red flush rose in his cheeks when he saw me.

"Hello," I said.

His breath froze in clouds. Snowflakes gathered in his hair. He waited, tensed, as if ready to spring away from me for good.

Oh, dear. Where to begin?

"You never finished my dancing lesson," I said.

His eyes narrowed. "Are you going to steal my purse?"

I nodded. "Probably."

He pressed his lips together and looked away.

The snow fell thick and fast now, blurring my view of him. I took a step closer.

"I promise never to rob anyone else, though."

His face broke into smiles. That one, glorious smile.

He reached down his hand.

I reached for his.

Epilogue

I hated to get out from under the warm sleigh wraps, but Gregor reached his hand to me.

Together we walked through the snow to where my house had stood, one day before.

Jets of steam still rose from a few places, though most of the wreckage had burned out and gone cold. Snow had begun to draw a blanket over charred metal and scorched stones, but in places where the fire still smoldered, sooty black spots yawned like gaping mouths.

Gregor watched my face. There were no tears to see today. Only snowflakes melting on my cheeks.

I looked up the hill to the garden. It was draped in white like a bridal veil, clothing even the Grecian lovers with some discretion.

"It was beautiful here," Gregor said.

"It still is."

He nodded.

A soft sound caught my ears, muffled and indistinct. I searched for the source of it. Running from the barns was Dog, plowing his way through the snow and sneezing when it caught in his beard.

With no regard for Louise's dress I knelt in the snow to embrace him. He placed his head over my shoulder and pressed his scratchy neck into mine. His loving bleat nearly deafened me.

At length I stood up again. Dog caught hold of my skirts in his teeth and began tugging me toward the remains of my house.

I let myself be led. Gregor's bewildered face wondered why.

"This goat is smarter than most people," I said. "More trustworthy, too."

We drew nearer to the ruins. "Careful," Gregor called. "Don't step on it."

As if understanding his words, Dog let go of my skirts and proceeded himself to clamber over the skeletal beams and mortared stone fragments. Debris shifted under his feet, and I nearly covered my eyes so as not to watch him collapse and fall into the cellars. But he treaded his way carefully over the mess, avoiding the hot areas. He bent and tugged at something, then carried it back to me in his mouth, dropping it at my feet.

I bent to pick it up. Gregor reached my side. I turned it over in my hands, staring.

"It's Beryl's pocket," I said. "The fabric isn't even singed."

Gregor poked at it. "That's like no fabric I've ever seen."

I nodded. "Hold out your hands."

Gregor cupped his two hands together, and I poured the contents of the pocket into them. His eyes grew wide.

They were the only bits of color in all this black-and-white landscape. Each like its own small sun, each color everlasting, as if they were droplets siphoned from the fountain where color first began.

"Just don't tell Peter about them," I said.

Beryl had more than kept her bargain. I would be a wealthy woman. I could rebuild my home. It would be a monument to my parents, and to Beryl, and I could live there without fear. I imagined it rising from these ashes like a phoenix.

But I would trade it all for Beryl, if she could come back and stay.

I bent low to scratch Dog's ears. "At least you're here with me, Doggy Goat," I told him. "You and I will remember her, won't we?"

As if in answer, he turned and trotted toward the wreckage once more, clambering over it until he reached the back of the house. Here he nosed through metal and rubbish more diligently. At last he *maaahed* to us. I hurried around the periphery to reach him.

Dog stood by a large earthenware butter crock, cracked and upended. I pulled at it with all my might until the debris pinning it yielded with a snap.

There, looking dejected in its pot, but certainly alive, was an amaranth flower.

Acknowledgments

First of all, everything is Phil's fault. If he hadn't been so encouraging, so enthusiastic, so eager to parent our boys while I wrote, none of this would have happened.

While it was happening, many talented writers carried me on their shoulders. I've been blessed by their good humor and encouragement. Cynthia Leitich Smith, Brent Hartinger, Tim Wynne-Jones, Carol Lynch Williams, Erik Talkin, Allyson Valentine Schrier, Kate Messner, and Ginger Johnson, I thank you and adore you.

I'm grateful to Michelle Nagler, whose inspired editing spared Lucinda and me many embarrassments; to Caroline Abbey, who made the way smooth; to Melissa Kavonic and Melanie Cecka, for shepherding the project along; to Jill Santopolo and Jandy Nelson, for wise and practical advice; and to Alyssa Eisner Henkin, a better ally than I deserve.

My flawless mother, Shirley Gardner, filled her home

with books and let me noodle my childhood away with them. Bless you, Mom, for that. Mary Vosler, my sterling sixth-grade teacher, insisted that writing be approached with great care. She shines in my memory. My sister Sally told me, after reading one of Mrs. Vosler's assignments, that I could be a writer someday. I believed her.

Joseph, Daniel, Adam, and David, my brilliant sons, are the reasons I write. But first and last, my loving husband, Phil, who continually clamors for more pages to read, deserves all the blame.